A NOVEL OF RES

M000314134

INTO THE RUBBLE

Based on a True Story

DOUGLAS DIETRICHSON

FREILING
PUBLISHING

Published by Freiling Publishing, a division of Freiling Agency, LLC.

70 Main Street, Suite 23-MEC
Warrenton, VA 20186

www.FreilingPublishing.com

ISBN 978-1-950948-27-7

DEDICATION

For Jackie, Jessica, Eric, Gabe, and Susannah.

On January 12, 2010, a devastating
earthquake struck Port-au-Prince, Haiti. The
author, who remains an active-duty fire
officer, responded as a Medical Specialist on
the team that was deployed by the United
States. The author writes this novel based on
his real-life experiences. He dedicates this
book to the thousands of victims, survivors,
and many rescuers that responded from
around the globe.

CONTENTS

CHARACTERS

Doug Dietrichson: Search and Rescue – Medical Specialist

Mark Murray: Police Flight Medic

Ron Shoemaker: Search and Rescue – Medical Specialist

Dr. Mike Hollaway: Search and Rescue – Medical Director

Dr. Bruce: Search and Rescue – Team Physician

Chief Mike Robinson: Search and Rescue – Plans Specialist

Chief Brian Tobias: Search and Rescue – Team Leader

Karen Lannigan: Search and Rescue – Ops Center Office Manager

Chief Kevin Markinson: Search and Rescue – Program Manager

Dan Barr: Search and Rescue – Red One Squad Leader

Evan Crandon: Search and Rescue – Red One Assistant Squad Leader

Earl Burrell: Search and Rescue – Rescue Specialist

Jim "Mack" McBride: Search and Rescue – Rescue Specialist

Riley Sutherland: Search and Rescue – Red Ops Chief

Heather Brecht: Search and Rescue Dog Handler

START OF A 72-HOUR-DAY

The twin-engine Bell helicopter flew north above 395 toward the Pentagon. Doug sat in the rear jump seat facing forward, looking out the port side window as the world passed below. The wall where American Airlines Flight 77 impacted and devastated the south side of the Pentagon on 9/11 came into view. This site was the place where Doug assisted young Defense Mortuary Affairs personnel, filling body bags with dead Americans.

Mark Murray, a veteran police officer, flight medic, and former classmate of Doug's at George Washington University's Emergency Management Program, watched him with a respectful silence. Flight banter ranged from discussions about stupid people and the job security they offer to their respective professions, or to who was dumber–firefighters or cops. But not on this flight. This flight was different. Mark recognized Doug's pensive look and left him to his thoughts.

Like most first responders, Doug was able to disconnect himself from the emotional and personal sides of dealing with such events. He never took joy in the misfortunes of others, but he didn't like to be left on the sidelines either. 9/11 was one of those days.

As they passed the Pentagon to the East, both Mark and Doug heard the earpieces in their flight helmets come alive.

"Eagle One from Base, you have been requested for a medevac on the George Washington Parkway. They have a car versus tree in northbound lanes. Standby for GPS coordinates."

"Copy Base, Northbound GW Parkway," Mark responded. "Do they have a landing zone (LZ) established for us?"

"That's affirmative Eagle One. They have the parkway shut down with LZ established one-quarter mile North of the scene. Go to Engine 18 for the LZ report on frequency 4 Hotel'."

"Copy Base," Mark repeated as he turned to look up at the pilot.

Mark could see that the pilot was talking to an air traffic controller on another frequency, and any interruptions on that frequency were strictly prohibited for anything short of telling him the rotor just fell off.

Mark waited until the pilot was finished before talking to him over the intercom.

"We have a mission. Northbound GW Parkway."

The pilot acknowledged Mark's message and turned north between Reagan National Airport and the Pentagon.

Mark reached above his head into a small compartment where he grabbed a pair of medical exam gloves and threw them at Doug.

"You might need these," Mark said.

"Thanks," Doug said, putting the gloves on. "I can use a pair of safety glasses, too, if you have an extra pair."

Mark stopped and looked at Doug as he was switching frequencies to talk to Engine 18.

"What is this – amateur hour?" Mark asked as he unzipped a lower leg pocket on his flight suit and pulled out safety glasses, flinging them at Doug with a little extra zip.

"Sorry," Doug said. "I thought we would get skunked like we always do."

Mark said nothing, but raised his eyebrows as if to say, "You never know now, do you?"

"Engine 18 from Eagle One, standing by for LZ and patient reports," Mark said over the radio.

"Copy Eagle One," Engine Eighteen responded. "No wires to report in the LZ area. If you are approaching from the south, you have trees to your three o'clock that will be in play within ten feet. We have one male patient with a decreased level of consciousness and severe lacerations to the upper left leg with arterial bleed and decreased breath sounds on the left with possible broken ribs and collapsed lung. Passenger is DOA."

Doug listened to the report as he watched Mark's face, which had no expression. He was unflappable. It was like he was listening to a waiter repeat what he just ordered at a restaurant.

"Copy Engine 18, arterial bleed and decreased breath sounds," Mark confirmed.

The officer on Engine 18 knew that the flight medic did not need the patient's whole medical history and date of last colonoscopy. Mark just needed enough for a general impression.

"Eagle One from Engine 18, I just got a report from Incident Command, and the patient has been extricated from the vehicle. They will load into the back of the medic unit and meet you at LZ. What's your ETA?"

"Three minutes out," Mark and Doug heard the pilot tell them over the intercom as he too was now listening in on the same frequency.

"On the ground in three," Mark confirmed, keying up the radio as he relayed the info to Engine 18.

The pilot slowed and started to descend as he made a 360 degree turn around the scene making sure the LZ was clear of any unseen obstructions.

They slowed to a hover as they approached.

"On final," both Mark and Doug heard the pilot say over the intercom.

"Copy, on final," Mark confirmed.

"On final," Mark repeated over 4 Hotel, the LZ frequency, which meant that there should be no radio traffic until they touch down, so the channel is free for the officer on the ground to call for an abort of the approach if required.

The helicopter touched down twenty feet in front of the medic unit, and both Mark and Doug jumped out with their gear and ran.

They climbed into the back where the field medics were working feverously on the patient. One medic was using a bag-valve-mask to assist with breathing, and the other was trying to control the bleeding.

"Do you have a tourniquet on?" Mark asked.

"Yeah!" the medic who was working on the bleeding, said incredulously.

"Ok, let's put a second one on then, and Doug, I need you to assess his lung sounds," Mark directed.

Doug grabbed his stethoscope and leaned down to listen. As he did, he looked at the trachea, where he noticed it was being deviated to the right.

"Hey Mark, I think we have a tension pneumothorax here," Doug informed Mark.

A tension pneumothorax would develop when a lung had

been punctured, and air became trapped between the chest wall and the lung. The increase in pressure, if strong enough, would force the trachea to shift. The trachea shift alone was not of great concern, but what it meant was. It indicated that the pressure was increasing in the chest, which would limit the amount of blood that could return to the heart.

"Mark, we need to needle his chest. I am barely getting breath sounds on this side with no radial pulse." Doug explained.

"Do it," Mark answered.

Doug asked for a chest needle as he started counting ribs. The landmark he was looking for was the third rib down, where he would insert the needle into the second intercostal space (space between the ribs).

After a quick wipe down to clean the area, Doug inserted the needle, which was followed by a gush of air.

"That sounds decompressed," Mark said as he heard the air rush out of the needle.

Mark continued, "We have the bleeding controlled. Let's get a one-way valve on that needle, so he doesn't suck air into his chest, and then get some IV fluids moving. After that, get another blood pressure then we can move."

It was a quick flight to the hospital where they were met by a team of nurses and surgeons in the trauma bay. Mark gave a detailed report of what they found, what they did, and what changed.

Mark and Doug returned to the helipad, where they took time to clean the gear and equipment.

"Well, Lieutenant, you do good work for a desk jockey," Mark teased.

Doug laughed.

"You know Mark, I can still get my gloves dirty anytime I want to by working overtime on weekends?"

"It must be nice to get that OT whenever you want. I guess they never came up with a cure for gluteus glaucoma?" Mark asked as he casually cleaned the stretcher down.

"Gluteus, what?" Doug asked, scrunching his face.

"You know... gluteus glaucoma. It's when firefighters can't see their asses going to work on weekends."

"Ok... ok..." Doug said, nodding his head in a defeated manner. "Would that be anything like the increased instances of color blindness among cops?" Doug asked.

"Now you are just making stuff up," Mark said as he started pushing the stretcher back to the helicopter, awaiting them on the helipad.

Doug had to suppress a laugh. "No, seriously. I mean, how else can you explain why cops always park in the yellow fire lanes at Dunkin Doughnuts?"

"Firefighters..." Mark said under his breath. "You have always been good at the comebacks," Mark said, putting the stretcher back in the helicopter and jumping in behind it. "Just for that, though, you can walk back to the hangar."

After touching back down at Base, Doug thanked Mark for the ride along and ran across the apron to his truck.

Twenty minutes later, Doug pulled into the parking garage at Public Safety Headquarters. It was a typical government building with a center core and offices along the outside walls. His office was modest in size with enough room for an ample desk with two computer monitors, a bookshelf that displayed all his Denver Broncos paraphernalia, and a small filing cabinet.

He had been promoted into his current position, Incident Reporting Administrator, approximately one-year prior on February 14th. That day held special meaning to him for other reasons as well. It was the same day he was given his jacket with a cross on it, certifying him as a ski patroller in 1992. That was a small miracle, considering how few times he actually had been skiing. That very evening was also his first date with Jackie, his wife, to be.

Doug was only twenty-one at the time. He had become an EMT just a year prior, after moving to Maryland from the small town of Iowa Park, Texas, where he grew up. He heard about a new ski resort being built in southern Pennsylvania, scheduled to open that winter. Doug, fancying himself a better skier than he actually was, called the mountain and asked if they were looking for ski patrollers. Since he was an EMT, he was hired immediately over the phone, but it eventually got cold enough to make snow, which meant it was time for the ski test. The lift towers were not in place yet, so all the prospective patrollers had to load up in the back of a truck, along with their skis, taking the access road to the top. Doug watched as the two patrol supervisors skied down and realized he had made a gross error in judgment. Doug was the first candidate to be evaluated. He made two turns, caught an edge, and went flying into the trees. After the ski test, they brought the candidates in one by one and gave them the results. When it was Doug's turn, they asked him how many times he had been skiing. He answered their questions, "Do you want me to include today? Because that would make it eight."

Lucky for Doug, his supervisors liked him and his work ethic to the extent they created a position for him known as trail crew. Although it was unspoken, Doug knew that his situation could also be known as: learn to ski, or you're fired. So that February 14th, in 1992, while on his first date with Jackie at the local patrol watering hole, Doug had to buy a round for the rest of the patrol. After the toast welcoming Doug into the ranks, the patrol director pulled Doug aside and asked him what he was thinking when he tried out for the patrol having so little ski experience. Doug's reply was simple: "You only asked me if I could ski. You didn't ask me if I was any good."

His phone was ringing as he entered his office, so he quickly dropped his satchel and hit the speakerphone.

"Good afternoon, Lt. Dietrichson." A very unhappy Chief began ripping Doug a new one.

"Have you found that report yet?" Chief asked.

"No, sir, I have not," Doug answered.

"Did you check the crew's tablet?" Chief asked.

"Yes sir, I did," Doug answered.

"And?" the Chief asked sarcastically.

"And what Chief?" Doug answered

"Was the report there?" the Chief continued. Doug put his elbows on his desk, rubbing his forehead in frustration.

"Chief, I just told you I couldn't find the report, and I might add, we were not losing reports like this before the update was pushed out," Doug said.

"Lieutenant, we went over this. IT said we had to push the update so we could see how it would work in a live environment. Apart from that, the medical examiner is calling to FOIA the report, and we don't have one," Chief said.

"And thanks to the live environment, the system is eating the reports. The crew told me they completed and posted the report to the server, and I believe them," Doug said.

Looking up, Doug noticed that his good friend Ron Shoemaker was standing at the door as the conversation started to heat up.

Ron quietly mouthed, "I can come back."

Doug didn't answer Ron but just stared at him shaking his head. Doug lifted his hand, making a blabbing motion and rolling his eyes, completely forgetting the Chief was still talking to him.

"Lieutenant Dietrichson, did you hear me?" the Chief snapped.

"Yes sir, I heard you... but you are starting to break up a little bit. Are you on a cell phone or in the elevator?" Doug asked.

Doug could hear the Chief just fine. "Chief, are you there?" Doug asked again.

"Lieutenant, can you hear me?" the Chief asked.

"Chief? Chief...?" Doug asked.

Click. Doug disconnected the call.

"He's going to figure that out one day, you know," Ron said as he walked in and sat in a chair next to Doug's desk.

Doug leaned back and let out a long, forceful exhale. "Ron, the guys in the field know this push was not my call, right?" Doug asked.

"Trust me, they know, but I won't lie to you either. The guys are pretty pissed about the system crashing and having to pull out the old paper forms," Ron answered.

"Tell me about it. The wife was pretty pissed off too. And to top that off, I had to leave the house at o' dark thirty to go the ER where medic units were stacking up because they couldn't finish their reports," Doug said.

Ron leaned forward, smacking Doug on the shoulder. "Doug, if you did nothing else, just being there in the middle of the night says enough," Ron said.

Doug leaned forward in his chair to fire up his computer and grab his stress ball. He didn't necessarily feel stressed, he just enjoyed bouncing it off the wall, especially when the Chief was in his office next door.

"Are you just getting into the office?" Ron asked.

"Yeah. I flew with Mark this morning," Doug answered.

"Get anything good?" Ron asked.

This question coming from a first responder meant just the opposite of good. It typically meant that it was the worst day of someone else's life.

"Actually, yeah. I had to dart someone's chest who dropped a lung. Don't get to do that one every day. What brings you into headquarters?" Doug asked.

"I had to pick up a new ID. Not sure why I even need it. The only reason I carry it is to get out of speeding tickets," Ron answered.

"Isn't that pretty much the only reason any of us carry it?" Doug said.

He paused and looked at what Ron was wearing. "Why are you in the Search and Rescue uniform?" Doug asked.

"Are you serious?" Ron said, surprised.

Doug just shrugged his shoulders. "Yeah."

"We have a drill today, you jack-ass!" Ron said.

"I thought that was tomorrow," Doug said, looking at his calendar. "Are we in the rubble pile or the rat's nest?"

"Neither. Cadaver lab," Ron answered.

Doug got a sour look on his face. "I hope they did a better job preserving this one than they did last time. I smelled so bad Jackie made me get undressed on the front porch."

"Can you blame her? We really stunk. Besides, she wouldn't let you get undressed in the bedroom...no matter what you smelled like," Ron said.

Ron laughed right up to the point where Doug threw his stress ball, hitting him in the forehead.

Ron stood up to retrieve the ball Doug had slung at him and took time to look at his Denver Bronco collection. "You know, you should have a real team like the Steelers," Ron said.

"You mean the Squealers?" Doug answered

"How did you become a Bronco's fan anyway growing up in Texas?" Ron asked.

"Well, I did grow up as a Cowboys fan, but it wasn't the same after Tom Landry. So, I was without a team for a year or so until the year of the drive, where Elway drove the distance of the field to score a touchdown for the tie, and then won in overtime."

"Is this Elway's rookie card?" Ron asked, still facing Doug's bookshelf.

"Sure is."

"Too bad you have it wrapped up. I need something to pick my teeth with," Ron said.

Doug wanted his stress ball back so he could throw it at Ron's head again.

"Yeah, ok, funny guy... Hey, what time does this drill start anyway?" Doug asked.

"1600," Ron said, looking at his watch.

Doug turned in his office chair to face Ron. "What do you say we leave a little early? It will put us ahead of 95 south traffic and get me out of here before the Chief gets back."

"Let's roll," Ron said.

Doug got up and pulled his search and rescue uniform off the hook from behind his door. As he was closing the door behind him, his phone started to ring again.

"Are you going to get that?" Ron asked, looking back into the office from the hall.

"No. I can forward the calls to my cell phone," Doug said.

"Did you forward the calls to your cell phone?" Ron asked.

"No," Doug answered.

Ron furrowed his eyebrows. "Well, doesn't that kind of make it impossible to answer then?"

"You're smarter than you look, Ron," Doug answered.

TOURNIQUETS FOR THE DEAD

Doug and Ron were accepted to Virginia Urban Search and Rescue team together as medical specialists (med specs) through a very competitive process. Team members were heavily vetted by their peers as well as the team's physicians. They both had paid their dues, being seasoned field medics, and both having worked as flight medics before joining the department.

Virginia Urban Search and Rescue team was one of two teams that were trained and equipped for international missions, with the other team located in California. Each team had abilities for responding to manmade and natural disasters such as bombings or hurricanes, etc. However, their expertise was in breaching and tunneling into occupied, collapsed structures and removing victims. Doug and Ron knew that while being on the team was voluntary, it was still a privilege not to be taken lightly that they were on the team the United States would send when other countries called for search and rescue assistance.

Their annual anatomy lab was held at a nearby medical school that gave the team access to their cadavers. The team physicians would put the guys on the team through their paces, challenging them with procedures ranging from surgical airways, inserting chest tubes, and field amputations.

Doug and Ron stood in the back of the class behind the other med specs. Dr. Mike Hollaway (Doc M.), the team's medical director, stood by the cadaver, demonstrating how to perform an amputation with a scalpel and a Gigli saw. Doc M had been with the team for a long time and had been on several deployments both domestically and internationally. And even though he was an attending physician at Georgetown University ER, he made the med specs feel like his equal. There was never a hint or undertone of "I am a doctor, and you are not."

"After you get down through the skin, use the scalpel to scrape away as much of the periosteum as possible. This will allow the Gigli saw to work more efficiently," Doc M. explained while he demonstrated the procedure on the cadaver's arm.

"Dude, this smells worse than the last one, Ron," Doug whispered.

"Yeah... guess you will be changing on the porch again?" Ron shot back.

Doug replied with a sarcastic laugh and a punch to Ron below the belt, causing him to double over, letting out a muffled groan.

Doc M. finished using the scalpel and was facing the med specs holding up the Gigli saw. It was a flexible wire saw with specialized teeth for cutting through bone structures.

"As you remember in our last anatomy lab, most of you were having trouble getting through the bone because you were holding the handles too close together. That creates a bad cutting angle and allows the teeth to get gummed up with bone tissue. You want to keep them further apart, which will allow for a cleaner cut and more cutting strength. Is everyone good on that? Does anyone have any questions?" Doc M. asked.

Doc M. made a study of Doug and Ron and knew they had not been paying full attention. "Doug and Ron, I have a victim up here with a 12×12 cement column laying across her legs, and she desperately needs them both amputated," Doc M. said.

Ron gave Doug a miffed look. "Way to go," Ron said.

The two of them started toward the table when Ron returned the same gut-punch to Doug. They positioned themselves on opposite sides of the anatomy table, where there were two small trays with various equipment necessary to complete their amputations.

Doc M. was known for making things interesting, especially during the full-scale exercises when tunneling through concrete, washing machines, refrigerators, or whatever they could pull out of the dump. His favorite antic was to pour a full can of chunky beef soup onto a student's head while they were trying to perform a procedure. Doug was his most recent victim. He was attempting to intubate a patient (a mannequin known as "Fred the Head") in a very confined space when down came the soup. "Hey Doug, looks like you need some suction down there," he heard Doc M. saying with a laugh as he watched from above.

"Alright, boys, we are going to have a friendly competition to see who can complete their amputations the fastest," Doc M. said, standing between Doug and Ron.

The chatter in the room grew louder with the anticipation of the contest.

Doc M. continued. "Hang on... hang on. We have some ground rules. This isn't like we are lopping off body parts with a reciprocating saw. It must be done correctly, in order, and safely. So, Doug and Ron, that means you cannot stab each other with scalpels to gain any advantage."

Doug and Ron shot each other disappointed looks.

"You will be on the clock, and time will stop when the lower leg is completely removed. We will assume that you have already started IVs and that you have sedated your respective patients. Go ahead and take a few seconds and make sure you have all your equipment, and it's ready to go."

Doug and Ron looked down at their trays and put their equipment in the order they would need them and then put on medical exam gloves and safety glasses.

Doc M saw they were done inspecting their equipment and gloved up and started the countdown. "Five, four, three, two, one–GO!"

Doug quickly worked his way down to the bone by making aggressive cuts with the scalpel. He pulled the muscle and skin back to get a better view. He then used the scalpel to scrape away the periosteum, as previously instructed by Doc M.

Ron began catching up as Doug was getting his Gigli saw into position.

"Remember your cutting angles," Doc M. reminded them.

Doug started sawing first and was making quick work of it.

Ron got his saw into place and began cutting through the bone, but it was not going to be fast enough.

Doug's Gigli was doing its work fast, and a few seconds later came free through the bone. Everyone in the lab started cheering and congratulating Doug as he held the amputated leg over his head in triumph.

A few moments later, Ron finished with his amputation and simply moved the leg aside.

Doug looked at Ron with a victorious smile, and Ron gave him a grin as if to say that he knew something that Doug did not. Doug's smile flickered a little, and he looked back down at the table to see if there was something he missed.

Doc M. put his hands up in the air, trying to get everyone to quiet down as he spoke over the cheering.

"Well done, well done! Much better technique used than last time, which was proved by the results and the time you did it in. Congratulations, Ron."

Doug did a double-take between Ron and Doc M. "Doc, I beat him by forty-five seconds," Doug said.

"You removed the leg forty-five seconds faster than Ron, but I said it had to be done in order," Doc M. reminded him.

Doug gave both Ron and Doc M. a confused look as he was trying to understand what exactly had happened. Ron just grinned.

"We usually put tourniquets on before we remove limbs, not after. Ergo, it has to be done in order." Doc M. said in a very matter-of-fact way.

Doug stared at the legs where one had a tourniquet, and the other did not. The lab erupted in laughter and jeering at Doug's expense. He took it in stride with a half-embarrassed smile.

After the laughter died down, Doug turned to Ron, "You would put a tourniquet on someone who's already dead."

The anatomy lab exploded in laugher again as Ron reached over and pulled Doug's ball cap down over his face.

"Ok, Doug came in second place in a two-man race, which means he gets to clean the lab when we finish up," Doc M. said, giving Doug a friendly pat on the back.

Later after the drill was complete and everyone had filtered out, Doug stood at the sink, rinsing off various tools such as clamps and bone saws. The door to the lab unexpectedly opened, and Dr. Bruce walked in. He was one of the other team physicians that Doug liked and respected. He was mild-mannered and easy to talk to.

"Hey Doc, I thought you left already," Doug said.

"Not yet. I was downstairs talking to Hollaway about next month's drill. You need any help in here?" Dr. Bruce asked.

Doug looked over his shoulder as he was placing a clean bone saw on a towel and motioned over to the table. "You can put her to bed if you like," Doug said.

Dr. Bruce walked over to the table and put on a pair of exam gloves. "How are the kids doing?"

"Ah, you know, they keep us busy," Doug said as he turned off the water and picked up a towel to dry the bone saw. "Actually, I should say that they keep Jackie busy. But I have to say that she is one stoic girl. She can go non-stop and sleep standing up."

"Does it bother you that she has to be so stoic?" Dr. Bruce asked, carefully placing one of the amputated legs back into its proper anatomical position.

"I don't really think about it," Doug answered.

"You don't?"

"I didn't mean it the way it sounded. Listen, Doc, it's just what her normal is. It's what our normal is," Doug said.

Dr. Bruce was carefully spreading a sheet back over the cadaver. "You know Doug, most couple's normal does not include three out of four autistic children," Dr. Bruce said.

"I'll give you that, Doc," Doug said as he continued to dry the bone saw. "But does it really surprise you when you consider who their father is?"

Doug walked over closer to the foot of the table where Dr. Bruce was standing.

"In all seriousness Doc, I do appreciate your concern for me, Jackie, and the kids. We just take it one day at a time and trust me, none of them are ever the same to be sure. But we rely a lot on prayer, faith, and friends. We just keep moving forward the best way we can."

"I guess that's all any of us can do, but if you need anything and Doug, I mean anything..."

Both Dr. Bruce and Doug were suddenly and eerily distracted as the leg Dr. Bruce put back on the table slumped over on its side, and the foot plopped out from underneath the sheet.

"That was really weird," Dr. Bruce said with a fixed gaze on the foot.

Doug shared the same look Dr. Bruce had as he stood motionless with the bone saw still in his hand.

"Which part? The fact she is dead or that her leg isn't attached?"

PORT-AU-PRINCE

Nadine was in a big hurry as she darted about the house, trying to get everything ready. It was a very humble place made primarily of cinder blocks and a metal roof, but it was their home, and they were grateful for it. Nadine was equally grateful that she had the opportunity to attend University, especially since sixty percent of the population of Haiti was educated only to the sixth-grade level.

Her mom, Liezel, watched her from a distance and attempted to calm her down. "Honey, you shouldn't worry so much. You have worked so hard; everything will be fine," Liezel said.

"Mom? Where is my backpack?" Nadine asked as her panic began to heighten even more.

Her mom was standing next to the kitchen table behind the chair, where she calmly picked up her backpack and set it on the table. "Sweetie, it's right where you left it five minutes ago," Liezel said.

Nadine swung around to see her backpack on the table with her mom behind it giving her a warm smile.

Her mom's smile broke her as she came to a stop, and her shoulders dropped.

"Ok, mom, you're right. I am a little panicked, but this project counts as half of our final grade."

"I understand, and again, it will be fine," Liezel said. Her mom walked over to her, placed her backpack over her shoulder, and grabbed her arms firmly with both hands. "Just look at my college girl. I am so proud of you. You will do great things as long as you believe in yourself."

Nadine stood in silence with an affectionate smile as her mom leaned forward and gave her a big kiss on her cheek.

A horn sounded from out in front of their house. Nadine quickly picked up a folded project board and kissed her mom.

"I have to go. I'll see you tonight," Nadine said.

Nadine ran out the front door and down to the street where an overcrowded tap-tap was waiting on her. There was no room to sit, so she jumped up on the bumper and grabbed hold of the makeshift handrail.

The tap-tap started to pull away as Nadine turned around and gave her mom a big smile.

"Wish me luck!" Nadine shouted back.

"Good luck, sweetie! I love you!" *There goes my college girl,* she thought to herself as she watched Nadine drive around the corner and out of sight.

***

On the other side of Port-au-Prince, Esther slowly walked up and down the aisles of the small, poorly stocked grocery store. She stopped and looked at the shelf where three loaves of bread remained. It was easy to look past the first loaf because it had too much mold. More than usual anyway, but she had become accustomed to simply trimming off the bad parts. The other two loaves had mold on them as well, but not so much she wouldn't be able to make them work for a small sandwich.

She placed the bread in her small cart and made her way to the counter, where a small woman sat upon a stool ready to ring her up.

"I hope you were able to find what you need. It is so difficult to get fresh groceries anymore," the cashier said.

Esther gave the cashier a conciliatory smile. "That's ok. I am happy I found what I could."

As Esther unpacked her groceries onto the counter, she noticed a small box with what appeared to be a single toy in it. "What is that?" Esther asked.

The cashier looked over the counter to see what Esther was referring to. "Oh, that. That is an army man with a parachute attached to him. You throw him in the air and whoosh, out comes the parachute, and he glides to the ground."

The cashier watched Esther as she looked at the price of the toy and back at her groceries.

"My little brother would love to have that, but maybe I'll get it next time if it's still here," Esther said.

"Actually, that has been sitting there for quite some time." The cashier prodded, "You take it. It needs a good home."

"I can't. It wouldn't be right," Esther said.

"I insist dear," the woman responded as she reached over and placed it into the bag with her other groceries. "See? Now I have more room on my counter," the cashier said.

"Thank you. That's very kind of you," Esther said.

"It's important that people help each other from time to time, is it not? Just like you are doing something nice for your little brother. Someday soon someone will do something to help you too. Wait and see," the cashier said.

The cashier finished placing Esther's groceries in a bag and handed them to her. "Next time you come, bring your little brother. Maybe I will have some candy for him and some bread with less mold."

Esther laughed. "Thank you again. I will bring my brother next time. He will want to thank you for his new toy."

"I look forward to it, dear. Have a nice day," the cashier said.

"You too," Esther answered as she turned to leave the store.

***

The Hotel Montana sat high in the hills of Port-Au-Prince. The art deco design was surrounded by endless palm trees and framed by tropical gardens. A large open terrace and pool positioned at the front allowed guests to relax with beautiful views of the bay far below, views enjoyed by the likes of actor, Brad Pitt, and former President Bill Clinton.

Adjacent to the terrace just inside, the hotel was a spacious lounge and bar where Claudette gave the bartender, Samuel, a drink order for her customers.

"I need three beers and a rum and coke," Claudette said.

"Ok, three beers and a rum and coke, but what do the customers want?" Samuel asked.

Claudette laughed. "I could use a strong drink about now."

"Why don't you take a day off? You work too much," Samuel said, pouring drinks.

"I can't afford to," she said, picking up a mixed drink order and placing it on her tray.

"Well, do me a favor and knock off early tonight. I can close up by myself," Samuel said.

Claudette picked up her tray and started toward the door going out to the terrace. "Maybe. I appreciate the offer, though."

She walked out to the terrace and over to a lounge chair where a female guest sat reading a book and placed the drink down on the table.

"Oh, there it is. Thank you," the guest said.

The guest took her sunglasses off and looked out over the bay.

"Isn't it just a beautiful day?" the guest asked.

Claudette looked out over the bay herself and shared the view with her guest. "Yes, I would have to agree."

"It's amazing from up here... you almost forget where you are," the guest added.

Claudette could only offer up a very patronizing, "Hmm, almost."

"Oh, where are my manners? Here you go, keep the change," she said, placing money on to Claudette's tray.

"Thanks..."

Claudette made her way back into the lounge, where she tossed her tray onto the bar.

"What's wrong?" Samuel asked as he was pouring a draft from the tap.

"Nothing three beers and a rum and coke can't fix," Claudette answered.

BURIED ALIVE

The tap-tap came to a stop in front of Port-au-Prince University. It wasn't the size of a typical university with a sprawling campus and numerous buildings. In fact, there was only one building on the campus and had the footprint the size of a four-story bank.

Nadine rushed up the front steps, dodging students as they were coming out the door, and she was going in. She zipped up the first flight of stairs where a boy tried to get her attention.

"Hey Nadine, do you ..." was all the boy could get out before Nadine ran past.

"Sorry. I'm in a hurry. Talk to you later," Nadine said.

As she reached the third floor, she found her classmates Mary and Stephanie waiting on her.

"I'm sorry," Nadine said as she gasped for air. "I tried to get here sooner, but..."

"Relax Nadine," her friend Mary said, trying to calm her. "Everything is ready to go."

"The charts? Where are the charts?" Nadine nervously asked.

"They are already in the classroom. You really need to relax," Stephanie said.

"I know. My mom keeps telling me the same thing," Nadine said.

Mary walked over to Nadine and put her arm around her. "Girl, we have this, and you carried us all the way. So, relax and just enjoy the moment."

Nadine nodded her head in agreement and let out a long sigh. "Yeah, you're right. We got this."

"Do me a favor and take my backpack? Mary asked. "I need to run downstairs to the restroom really quick."

"Ok, but don't be late," Nadine yelled after her as Mary started toward the stairs.

"She won't be late," Stephanie said as she grabbed Nadine's arm and pulled her toward the classroom.

The two of them walked together with confident smiles on their faces as they heard a low rumble and felt the floor move beneath them. They both stopped and looked at each other, and their confident smiles were replaced with fear.

"What's happening?" Nadine shouted.

Stephanie grabbed Nadine by her arms as she struggled to keep her balance.

As Mary was running down the stairs, they began to shift, throwing her up against the railing. She looked out the large windows on the front of the building as they suddenly shattered into a million shards and rained down on terrorized students as they attempted to flee the building.

Nadine and Stephanie screamed as the third floor violently shook and started to shear apart, causing all the windows around them to burst. Several large pieces of the floor separated, giving way underneath them. Stephanie lost her footing and began sliding down into the gaping hole that was left as Nadine did not let go of her and followed her into the dark emptiness as large pieces of concrete, ceiling, and roof followed behind them.

Mary was violently thrown from the railing back against the wall of the stairway. The top landing and the bottom landing of the stairs were torn away with such force, Mary and the staircase were momentarily suspended in midair together before they both disappeared into a billowing cloud of grey dust.

***

Claudette glared out the windows of the lounge toward the terrace. The obnoxious guest was living rent-free in her head, which just made her even more frustrated. She shook it off and turned to pick up a beer in a frosted mug waiting to be delivered to a table when it started to vibrate away from her. Startled, she pulled her hand back as the other beer-filled mugs began to do the same. Her eyes met with the bartender, who was equally unnerved.

What was a vibration suddenly intensified as glasses and liquor bottles crashed down onto the counters behind the bar. Both Claudette and Samuel grabbed the bar to keep their balance. Guests in the lounge jumped from their bar stools and chairs and ran over each other, trying to make it to one of the exits.

As Claudette continued to hold onto the bar, she saw large pieces of concrete falling from above and smashing onto the terrace. A moment later, the ceiling in the lounge gave way, and concrete and objects from the floor above came crashing down.

Samuel started to make a run for Claudette. "We have to get out of here! Go! Go!" he screamed.

As soon as Claudette let go of the bar to start running, the floor broke away from underneath her feet, and she began to fall backward. Samuel dove for her headfirst.

"Claudette!" Samuel yelled.

He was not able to reach her before she fell into the rubble and darkness. As fast as Claudette disappeared, the floor above came crashing onto Samuel, violently forcing him down to his grave below.

***

Esther reached in her bag and pulled out her brother's new toy as she stood just outside the store. *He will be so happy to get this,* she thought to herself.

A large truck drove by as she was putting the toy back

in her bag, and she felt the vibrations from it under her feet. It was one of those passive sensations she typically wouldn't give a second thought to until Esther realized the truck had disappeared down the street, and those same vibrations were still underfoot and getting worse.

She looked up at the buildings across the street and saw them swaying back and forth as she was struggling to keep her feet underneath her. She became paralyzed by terror as she watched the walls of the buildings begin to splinter, and cracks ran in every direction as they started to crumble under their own weight.

People were jumping out of third, fourth, and fifth story windows to the ground below landing on the sidewalk and other people who were attempting to flee. Then one by one, the floors of buildings collapsed onto each other in a pancaked effect crushing people who were only inches from safety.

Esther was so gripped by the inhumanity unfolding before her she failed to recognize her own mortal danger. The roof of the porch she stood on was supported by large columns that began to disintegrate around her. Esther suddenly pitched backward as the building she just left started to collapse, and the columns came crashing down one by one. In a final effort to escape, she dove forward with all her strength with her arms stretched out in front of her. She was only a few feet from reaching the street when a cement column from the porch came down on top of her striking her on the right shoulder as they both vanished into a grey plume of dust.

Forty-five seconds after the quake began, Haiti laid in ruins.

BUSTED

Doug turned left down his street as Toby Keith was getting to the good part, '*Cause we'll put a boot in your ass. It's the American Way.* Even though Doug's guitar repertoire consisted of a mean G chord and only the G chord, he imagined himself a natural likeness to Toby Keith. However, when it came to singing, he had a silky smooth baritone voice of a Brad Paisley. At least that's what Doug heard anyway...

The Dietrichson's lived in a modest two-story cape cod, which backed up to the woods along Quantico Marine Corps Base. Doug enjoyed the proximity because he liked to listen to the automatic gunfire and heavy munitions going off, and now and again, he could see Marine One flying over.

The dash on his truck showed an outside temperature of twenty degrees. So, the plan was to sneak up to the porch, quietly take off his boots, and get up to the shower before he could get caught by Jackie. He was not going to get undressed outside again, not in those temps.

The linchpin would be getting the door unlocked without

Reagan, his four-year-old American Brittany, giving his presence away. He got up to the porch and got his boots off. So far, so good. Setting his backpack down, he fished out his house key and slowly inserted it into the lock, turning it as it made a crisp clicking sound. Nothing but silence came from the other side of the door. *I should have been a Navy Seal.*

Turning the handle, he slowly opened the door, which came to a sudden stop as the chain on the other side jerked tight with enough sound for Reagan to hear.

Busted, Doug thought to himself as Reagan started barking from the other side of the door.

Doug just stood there with his eyes closed. When he opened them, Jackie was standing there like an apparition, appearing from nowhere.

"Oh, hey, babe. I was just about to call for you. Can you take the chain off, please? It's a little cold out here," Doug said.

"No," Jackie answered.

"C'mon. Stop playing around," Doug demanded.

"No," she repeated.

"Jackie, I'm not kidding," Doug remarked seriously.

"No."

"I have my keys and can get to the basement door before you and just come in that way," Doug said.

"Chained and locked," Jackie replied without emotion.

"Did Ron call you?" Doug wondered aloud.

"Maybe."

"I'll slash his tires!" Doug exclaimed. "Ok, Babe, how about this..."

"Strip," Jackie said, interrupting Doug.

"What?" Doug said, stunned.

"Strip," Jackie repeated.

"If you actually think I am going to strip down out here in this weather you..." was all Doug could get out before the door shut in his face.

Doug let out a long sigh as he knocked on the door. A few moments later, his six-year-old daughter Susannah opened the door.

"Hi, Daddy," Susannah said.

"Hey, Boo. Daddy is cold out here. Can you undo the chain so I can come in and get a warm hug from you?" Doug cajoled.

"Mommy said strip," was all she said before the door closed again.

As he was getting ready to bust the door off the hinges, Jackie opened it back up and thrust something out at him.

"Bag them," Jackie said.

Doug snatched the black trash bag out of her hand. "When I am done, the chain comes off the door, right?" Doug asked.

"Yes," Jackie replied evenly.

Doug pulled off his job shirt and tossed it into the bag, followed by his tee-shirt, muttering not so nice things about Ron while doing so.

As Doug undid his belt, pulling his pants down, Jackie extended her hand out the door and waved at the neighbors.

"Oh look, it's the Whites. Hi Dianna. Hi Andrew," she said pleasantly.

Doug just rolled his eyes. "You actually think I am going to fall for that?"

"Hi, Jackie. Did he have another anatomy lab today?" Dianna asked.

Jackie held her hand over her mouth, trying not to laugh out loud.

Doug was done. He had nothing. "Can I please come inside and take a shower?"

***

Jackie was in the kitchen cooking one of everybody's favorite throw-down meals, kielbasa with mac and cheese. The sauce for the kielbasa comprised of brown sugar and mustard. That was it, seasoned to taste. It was an easy meal that Doug used himself when cooking at the fire station. The only exception was that the mac and cheese had to be real cheese and not the powdered crap.

Jackie called out to their oldest daughter Jessica who was eleven. Jessica came into the kitchen and stood in silence next to Jackie but would not look at her. It was her way to let Jackie know she was ready to listen.

"Can you please go tell Daddy dinner is ready?" Jackie asked.

"Daddy, dinner is ready." Jessica echoed.

"Thank you, sweetie."

This was a very common exchange with their oldest three children, especially Jessica. Autistic children struggle with social cues, mannerisms, and facial expressions, which is why Jessica seldom made eye contact. Facial expressions just confused her very black and white world, which was vexing enough. So why bother looking at people?

This also made for very literal translations, about which Doug had to be careful. If he said, "I would love to launch the neighbor's cat into the woods!" Jessica's mind would envision her father in the backyard using a catapult, pun not intended, launching Fluffy over the trees until it appeared only as a small black dot sailing off into the horizon.

Eric, who was nine, and Gabe, seven, shared space with Jessica on the spectrum as well. They were a little more expressive and welcoming into their individual worlds. It was tough for Doug and Jackie to navigate what was an invite and what wasn't. Just because they would sit in silence, in their own little worlds, you could never assume they were not acutely aware of what was happening around them. This was especially so with Jessica. They quickly realized that within their perceived weaknesses also existed unveiled strengths.

Doug was enjoying his hot shower when the door to the bathroom opened almost simultaneously, with the shower curtain pulling back.

"Daddy, dinner is ready."

Doug scrambled to pull the shower curtain back over himself.

"Ok, thank you, Schmoopie."

Jessica turned and started to walk back out the door.

"Hey, Schmoopie, can I get a big fish kiss?" Doug asked.

Jessica did a one-eighty and came back to Doug, where she stood with big pursed lips and eyes closed. Doug leaned down and did the same, giving her a big kiss.

"I love you, Schmoopie."

"Love you," Jessica said, walking out of the bathroom, leaving the door open behind her. Doug laughed. He loved his quirky children.

Jackie was finishing up dinner in the kitchen, where she had the small, countertop TV on listening to the news.

"A major earthquake rocked the impoverished Caribbean nation of Haiti today at approximately 4:53 local time. Haiti is the poorest nation in the Western Hemisphere. With poor infrastructure, officials greatly fear that the death toll could reach into the tens of thousands, if not more."

Just as Jackie was turning to watch the coverage on the earthquake, the telephone rang.

Back upstairs, Doug stood in front of his closet, wearing flannel pants and a sweatshirt when he turned to see Jackie standing there with the phone.

"I was just on my way down. Is that for me?" Doug asked.

"Yeah. It's Dr. Hollaway."

"It's probably about the drill today," Doug said as he took the phone from her.

"Hey, Doc, what's up?"

Doug stood listening for a few moments, and Jackie could see the expression changing on his face.

"Yeah, I'm pretty sure I can. Where is Port-Au-Prince?" Doug asked.

"Haiti," Jackie said with a blank stare.

YOU WERE APPOINTED FOR THIS

Chief Mike Robinson, who was a Plans Specialist, sat at a desk in the team's operations center, which was located in a building next to the fire academy. As he sat there with the phone in one hand, he used the other to rest his forehead in as he leaned on the desk.

"No, I understand, Colonel. But sir, let me ask you this. Would there be any advantage if we drove to Dover and loaded from there?" Mike asked.

Mike turned to see Chief Brian Tobias, team leader, walking into the Ops Center. It was evident to Brian that Mike did not like what he heard on the other end of the phone.

"Eight hours. I didn't realize they needed that much downtime between flights. Ok, well, thank you, Colonel, for your time, and please contact us if that status changes. Yes sir, good night," Mike said, hanging up the phone.

"Doesn't look like we will be flying Air Force this time, Brian. They have a C-5 on its way back from the Middle East to Dover, but they are still six hours out and have a mandatory eight-hour downtime after landing," Mike explained.

"C-17s?" Brian asked.

"I asked about those too, and they don't have any available," Mike answered.

"Well, we have two wars going on, so military cargo planes are at a premium. But let's keep this in perspective by remembering what those C-5s are carrying back to Dover," Brian said.

"Amen to that," Mike said in agreement.

Mike and Brian were both, in their own rights, a couple of Cool Hand Lukes. Nothing ever seemed to phase them, no matter how difficult a situation got. They could be incident commanders on a high-rise fire with mothers tossing their babies out windows, and they would casually direct personnel where to go catch the next one without a hint of panic in their voice. Most importantly, they had the respect of the men and women in the field. Mike and Brian trusted the people in the field; therefore, they trusted them. It was a simple concept.

Karen walked into the office and handed Brian a piece of paper.

"Here is an updated roster for you, Chief. We are still

working with operations to find relief for the other members that are still on duty," Karen said.

"Thanks, Karen," Brian replied as he made a quick study of the roster.

Karen was a civilian that worked for the team and was the glue that kept things from unraveling. She understood the program better than most of its members and was a vital piece to the team's success.

"Karen, can you please let me know when the command and general staff have arrived so we can get a quick brief done?" Brian asked.

"Yes, sir." And just as if she was reading his mind, "I went ahead and started a fresh pot of coffee," Karen said.

"I love you, Karen," Brian said.

"I love you too, Brian," Karen playfully said as she walked away.

Making coffee was not part of her job description, but it's just the type of person she was.

"She is always three steps ahead of us, isn't she Mike?" Brian said, smiling.

"Good thing too. We would be lost without her," Mike said.

"Have you heard from Chief Markinson?" Brian asked, looking at the roster.

"He just landed at Dulles and is on his way over here right now. Until he gets here, I am going to get back on the phones and start working on our civilian contacts for a commercial C-130 for the cache and a charter flight for the team," Mike said.

"Mike, please let them know that this is a very fluid situation, and we will need a lot of flexibility on this one," Brian said.

"Fluid? Brian, I'm not sure we even have an airport to land at in Haiti," Mike answered.

"I don't care if we have to do a water landing and swim to shore. Time is critical here, and we need to touch down in Haiti," Brian said.

"Roger that Brian," Mike said.

***

They pulled into the fire academy parking lot a little past 2030. Doug had already had a long day, and yet he felt like it was just getting started.

It was a quiet ride in for them as Susannah and Eric were already asleep, and Gabe and Jessica were tucked away in their own little worlds. Doug pulled their E350 into a parking space and turned off the van.

"Ok Jackie, I need to know about this one. I can tap out if you need me to," Doug said

"We went over this. I am fine. The kids are fine. We're good," Jackie replied.

Doug stared out the front windshield watching other families say bye to team members as they were dropping them off. Jackie could tell he was having his doubts but would have even more regret for not going.

"You need to do this. I'm not saying that it's something you need to get out of your system. It's just what you do, and you are good at it. Those poor souls are in need, and you are appointed to be there," Jackie said.

Doug continued staring out the front of the van, gradually nodding his head as he turned to Jackie. "You're right," Doug said.

"I know I'm right. Besides, you would drive me nuts being home with the team gone."

As Doug was looking at Jackie, he could tell she was distracted by someone behind him.

"Hey Jackie," Ron said, walking up to the van.

"Hi, Ron. Did Laura drop you off?" Jackie asked.

"No. I drove myself. It was just easier," Ron said as he was poking his head in to see who else was in the van. "Did you bring the pack with you?"

"We sure did," Jackie said, turning around to look at the kids. "Tell Mr. Ron, hi."

"Hi, Mr. Ron," the kids said all together.

"By the way, thanks for the head-up earlier today," Jackie said with a smile.

Doug did a double-take between Jackie and Ron.

"Oh yeah. I didn't get a chance to thank you either, Ron," Doug said, reaching out the window to flick Ron extra hard on the ear.

Ron flinched and grabbed his ear. "Ow."

"I already have my stuff in. Do you want me to grab some of your gear and bring it to check-in?" Ron asked Doug.

"Umm, sure. Thanks, buddy. I'll be there in a few minutes."

Ron turned to go to the back of the van and grab some gear, and Jackie called out after him.

"Ron, take care. Be safe over there," Jackie said.

"We will. Thanks, Jackie."

Doug got out of the van and walked over to the passenger-side, double-doors so he could get hugs.

"Alright, kiddos. Daddy must take a little trip. I need you guys to be good for Mommy, ok?"

Gabe perked up when he heard Doug say be good for Mommy. "Good for Mommy," he repeated.

"That's right, buddy. Ok, you guys can unbuckle and get out so I can give you a big hug and kiss," Doug said.

One by one, they hopped out, except for Jessica, who was still staring out the window.

Doug gave Eric, Gabe, and Susannah a big hug and kiss. "I love you guys and will miss you every minute."

"Love you, Dad," they all said together.

He turned to get into the back of the van and knelt beside Jessica's seat. "Hey, Schmoopie, Daddy has to go away for a little while on a trip."

"Daddy going on a trip," Jessica echoed as she kept staring out the window.

Doug watched her as she continued to stare out the window, and he started to get choked up, not because he was leaving, but rather he wondered if they would ever be together in the same world at the same time, whether it's his or hers.

"I love you, Schmoopie-head," he said as he got up to give her a long kiss on top of her head.

"Love you," Jessica said without turning to see him leave.

Doug slowly got out of the van and shooed the others back in. "Alright, back in your seats, munchkins. Buckle up."

Doug closed the doors and turned to Jackie. "Do me a favor and give Lisa, Donnie, David, and Amy a call and let them know I am deploying – especially David. He will have a thousand questions as usual. Call Bucko too and let him know I will not be ski patrolling for a few weeks."

"Got it. Anything else?" Jackie asked.

"No, I think that's about it. I should get in there to give Ron a hand at medical check-in."

Doug gave Jackie a big hug and kiss. "Love you," Doug said.

"Love you too. Be careful over there. Don't do anything stupid."

Doug laughed. "You know me. I'm a soul of caution."

"Uh, huh," Jackie said sarcastically.

Doug gave Jackie one last hug and a quick kiss on the forehead.

"I'll see you soon," Doug said as he turned and walked into the academy.

Jackie called out to Doug just as he was about to pass through the doors, "Remember Philippians 4:13."

Doug stopped and turned around to look at her, giving her a nod, "You're right...4:13. I love you."

He blew her one last kiss and disappeared into the academy.

RED SQUAD ONE

Doug made his way inside to a large room where team members were getting processed for deployment. He found Ron sitting behind a table with a stethoscope around his neck, filling out paperwork for the medical check-in.

"Sorry about that. It went a little longer than planned," Doug said.

"No worries," Ron said as he continued to fill out paperwork. "Doc M. just stopped by and wants us asking the team to make sure they have enough of their medications for up to a month-long deployment."

"One month, huh?" Doug said as he was putting a stethoscope around his neck and fishing out a pen from his BDU pocket.

"Yeah. Apparently, it's worse than what they are showing on the news right now."

Doug and Ron continued checking-in their team members when someone tossed down their paperwork onto the table in front of Doug. Doug looked up, half annoyed until he saw who it was.

"Mack! My brother from another mother! They letting you go on this one? We must be scraping the bottom of the barrel," Doug said.

Mack just laughed. "You got that, right!"

It was impossible to get a dig in on Mack. He was shameless but hilarious. What made him so amusing was the moments when he was not trying to be. It's just who he was.

"Hey, did you see the roster yet?" Mack asked as he was pulling a piece of paper out of his pocket.

"No. Not yet," Doug said.

"Me and you on Red Squad One, baby!" Mack exclaimed.

Doug took the roster from Mack and read it. "Wow, we are stacked. Dan is the squad leader, Evan is assistant squad leader, you, and Earl. Oh, and look, Dan's BFF Riley is Red Ops. You know he will find us some work over there," Doug said.

"You know it," Mack said with a big smile.

Doug handed the roster back to Mack and started looking over his medical sheet.

"They want us asking everyone if they have enough medications for a one-month deployment," Doug asked Mack.

"Unless I need to bring enough Gas-X for both of us, I should be good," Mack answered.

Both Doug and Ron laughed.

"Yeah, yeah... I hear you, funny guy." Doug shook his head, "Take a seat so I can get your blood pressure."

While Mack was sitting down to get his blood pressure, Chief Robinson entered the room. "Listen up, everyone," he instructed. "There will be a full team briefing in thirty minutes–thirty minutes."

The team wrapped up the check-in process about fifteen minutes later, and for the most part, had gathered into their respective squads. From that point until they returned from their deployment, everything would be done as a squad.

There were four squads in total, two red and two blue known as Red One, Red Two, Blue One, and Blue Two. The squad positions were filled by career firefighters that worked for the fire department. Many of them were cross-trained in other specialties. To that end, it was not unusual to see a medical specialist pick up a jackhammer or chipper and go to work, or a rescue specialist start an IV on a victim if they were in a better position than the medic specialist when it needed to be done. There were also civilians on the team, such as physicians, search dog handlers, and structural engineers. The squads were a great source of indigestion for the structural engineers because they often breeched or tunneled their way into places that defeated the purpose of the engineer being on the team to begin with.

Doug was pleased that he was placed in the squad he was. Dan Barr, the squad leader, was a good decision maker and didn't need an ops manual in front of him to make one either. He took each situation for what it was and simply worked the problem and was willing to push the limits. Not that he was necessarily a rule-breaker, but he was not scared to cross that line when needed. Evan Crandon was the assistant squad leader and just an all-around good guy who genuinely cared about people. He was quiet and mild-mannered, but one of the hardest workers on the team. Earl Burrell was kin to Sam Elliot's character in *We Were Soldiers*. He was a bit gruff on the outside and a teddy bear on the inside, but he just always sounded like a gruff. Earl was another hard worker and a total team player. Jim McBride, who everyone called Mack, was a magnet for crazy situations. Again, a real hard worker and strong as an ox. The only hang-up that Mack really had was his food. He couldn't stand eating Meals Ready to Eat (MREs), so he always stashed peanut butter and jelly in his bag, along with a few loaves of bread. The other part of that hang-up was Mack didn't like people messing with his food. So naturally, someone would always put their finger in the middle of his sandwich when he wasn't paying attention.

As the squads continued their individual meetings, the team's program manager, Chief Kevin Markinson, entered the room. He was a carbon copy of that guy on Mr. Clean commercials. Chief Markinson was a strong leader and was not scared to admit when he did not have an answer, but he would make sure he would find one. He always said that the key to good leadership was to surround yourself with people smarter than you and listen to them, and when things go right, they get the credit, but if they go bad, you do. Everyone respected him.

He met briefly with Doc M, Brian Tobias, and Mike Robinson at the front of the room, where they all stood behind a podium. A few moments later, Chief Markinson addressed the team. "All right, team, listen up. As all of you are already aware, a very shallow 7.0 earthquake struck Haiti today a few minutes before 1700 local time. The area of Port-au-Prince was hit the hardest. We have confirmation that the casualties are high, and the local infrastructure has already been overwhelmed in every manner imaginable."

Shallow earthquakes typically cause more damage as opposed to deeper ones. The deeper ones have to travel further to the surface and lose energy along the way.

Chief Markinson continued, "I just got off the phone with our ambassador in Haiti, and they have received minimal damage there, so unless anything changes, the embassy will be our base of operations (BOO). We will be letting your families know that each evening there will be a teleconference from the ops center at approximately 1800 to keep them informed of your activity and movement."

As Chief Markinson finished speaking, Brian Tobias approached the podium. "First off, there is a lot of information coming in, and it is always changing, so we ask you to remain patient and flexible. So, first things first, getting there. We recently learned there is still an outside chance of getting a C-17, but it's an outside chance at best. Plan B is we will be going over on a chartered 737, and the cache will follow close behind on a commercial C-130. If that happens, we will likely be up through the night at Dulles Airport, splitting the cache because it will not all fit. That means recon, technical search, and medical gear go first, along with food and water. On that note…"

Brian reached down under the podium and grabbed a bottle of water and an MRE and held it up. "Your meals should come out of a bag that looks like this. If not, don't eat it. Same for the water. If it doesn't look like this, don't drink it. Am I clear on that?"

The team all acknowledged in unison. "Yes, sir."

He paused for a few moments studying the faces in the room as he collected his thoughts on what he wanted to say next."Those of you who were at the Pentagon on 9/11 are familiar with the sights, sounds, and smells that come with this job."

The room fell completely silent as the team sensed the seriousness of Brian's words. "Ladies and gentlemen, I am going to be completely honest with you. Even though 9/11 happened in our own backyard, I feel this will be worse."

HEADING FOR WARMER WEATHER

The sun started to rise over Dulles Airport as the team finished separating the cache out on the tarmac. Mack had his arms tightly wrapped around his chest with his chin tucked into his coat, trying to keep warm.

"Dan, I'm freezing my nuggets off," Mack said.

"I wouldn't worry too much about that, Mack," Dan said. "I feel confident that it will change for all of us by this afternoon. Go see if Red Two is finished with that pallet jack and help Doug and Earl get this loaded onto the plane. That will help keep you warm."

Across the tarmac, standing in front of a large hangar, Chief Markinson, Brian, Mike, and Karen gathered in a small circle.

Karen handed Brian a plastic file box. "Here are the passports and the member files. Also, a group email was sent out thirty minutes ago to the families with all the information they need for the teleconference tonight."

"Thank you, Karen," Brian replied.

"Brian, try to get us a SIT REP as soon as you can from over there," Chief Markinson said, trying to talk over a 737, being marshaled to a stop behind the C-130.

"Will do. It looks like our ride is here," said Brian.

"Brian, when I get back to the ops center, I will put a roster together for another team to be ready for a domestic deployment or to send down to you if needed," instructed Kevin.

"Sounds good, Kevin," Brian replied.

Riley Sutherland, the Red Ops chief, approached Brian as Karen finished hugging him and wishing him good luck. "Brian, the team is ready to load."

"Copy. The cache has been secured?" Brian asked.

"All ready to go," Riley replied.

"Good. Go ahead and start loading the team. I'll see you on the plane," Brian said.

As Riley turned to get the team going, Brian reached out to Chief Markinson to shake his hand.

"Great job getting the team out the door. You too, Karen."

"It was a team effort," Kevin reminded him. "A team effort," he repeated, giving Brian a friendly wink. "Be safe over there, but save as many as you can."

"Thanks, Chief. We'll do our best."

Brian and Mike picked up their packs and headed for the air stairs positioned next to the 737, where the team was finishing getting loaded up. Brian was the last one up the airstairs where he stopped at the top before boarding, turned, and gave Chief Markinson and Karen a confident thumbs up.

***

Nelson was driving home when the earthquake hit. The road under his car buckled and splintered, causing him to crash into the wall that surrounded the Port-au-Prince University.

He was able to get out of his car before the wall broke apart and crashed through his windshield. The students that were in the building were not as lucky.

Nelson was up all night, along with many others who stopped to help. Sadly, the number of deceased victims they pulled out was much greater than those they pulled out alive. They stacked the bodies behind the collapsed building.

Nelson knew there were many more in there, and he simply did not have the ability or resources to get to them. But he was determined to rescue as many as he could.

Those he was working with decided it would be helpful to move further into the rubble pile and continue calling out. Even if they were not able to reach them, they could at least mark areas where they knew victims were.

He made his way to the top of a building that once stood forty feet high and now was a twenty-five-foot-high pile of busted concrete.

"HELLO! CAN ANYONE HEAR ME? HELLO!" Nelson yelled out.

Twenty feet below where Nelson stood, Stephanie lay trapped under a large slab. She began to stir and slowly open her eyes. As Stephanie tried to move, severe pain shot through her left leg that was trapped. She cried out in agony.

Nelson froze. He knew he had heard someone. "HELLO! CAN YOU HEAR ME?"

Stephanie lifted her head, almost forgetting about her pain. She tried to focus through the darkness while wiping pebbles and dust from her eyes. She could make out from the small amount of light that she lay trapped in what appeared to be a small cavern.

"HELLO? IS SOMEONE THERE? I'M DOWN HERE! DOWN HERE!" She screamed.

Nelson heard someone. He turned and ran over to where there was an opening that looked down into a large void space. "I HEAR YOU! I'M HERE!"

Stephanie started weeping. "Oh, thank you, God. Thank you."

"What is your name?" Nelson called down to her.

"Stephanie! My name is Stephanie," she called back.

"Ok, Stephanie. My name is Nelson. Are you trapped? Can you move?"

Stephanie took the time to assess how exactly she was trapped. "My leg is pinned under a large piece of concrete. I think it's broken. The rest of the concrete is laying on top of something else. I can move my arms and upper body."

"Is there anyone else near you?" Nelson asked.

She peered around as much as she could, straining her neck to look across to the other side of the vast void. She saw Nadine lying on her back, trapped under a slab that covered the left side of her body. "NADINE! CAN YOU HEAR ME? NADINE!" Nadine remained motionless as Stephanie began weeping again.

"Do you see someone else down there?" Nelson asked

Stephanie tried to answer. "I...I see my friend, but she isn't moving."

Daniel could hear Stephanie weeping.

He waited several minutes before talking to her again. "Stephanie, we know where you and Nadine are now, and I am not going to leave you, ok? I will stay right here, and when help comes, I will tell them where you are. Ok?"

"Thank you, Nelson. Thank you."

NO PASSPORTS NEEDED

The 737 flew over the island at 5000 feet, making a big sweeping turn back toward the airport giving the team a view of all the damage below. Those on the opposite side of the plane clambered over to the other to jockey for window space. The team was stacked on each other like sardines leaving absolutely no one on the other side of the aircraft.

Doug had an inkling that it was going to be bad based on everything the team had been told up to that point; however, he didn't think it would be as extensive as what he saw through the window.

Mack was sitting in the row in front of Doug, sharing the same stunned expression the rest of the team wore.

"It looks like there are more houses on the ground than there are standing," Mack said.

"I hoped you packed plenty of PBJ Mack. It looks like we will be here a while," Doug said with his stare still fixed out the window.

Their plane touched down and taxied over to an open

hangar where a single Haitian official awaited them. After the aircraft shutdown, the airstairs were quickly put into place, and the official boarded the plane.

Brian stood to meet him.

"Thank you so much for you and your team coming so quickly. Much help is needed," the official said, shaking both their hands firmly.

"Yes, sir. You are quite welcome. I am Brian Tobias of Virginia Urban Search and Rescue, and this is Mike Robinson."

Brian lifted the file box with the team's passports and started to hand them to the official. "Sir, I have our pass..."

"That won't be necessary," he said, cutting him off. "I have a place for you and your team over here in the hangar to wait. Come..."

Brian turned to Mike. "That's the fastest I have ever made it through customs in any country."

Once the whole team was off the plane, Brian circled them up for a quick brief.

"Listen up," Brian started. We are going to stage here until the C-130 arrives, which is still one hour out. We are working on getting a forklift to get the pallets off the plane and onto a truck that is currently on its way from the embassy. That gives you one hour to grab a power nap. You're going to need it. Before we break, I need to meet with both Red and Blue Recon, and technical search team managers for a couple of minutes."

Red One found some floor space under the wing of an old aircraft, where they dropped their packs on the floor and laid down. Even though most of them had been up for over twenty-four hours, they were too amped-up to get any meaningful rest.

During the downtime, Doc M. and Dr. Bruce made their way around to all the med specs and handed them their NARC packs. The NARC packs were controlled substances such as pain medicine like Fentanyl, and sedation drugs like Ketamine, which the med specs called vitamin K.

Exactly one hour later, the C-130 landed and taxied over to where the flatbed truck was waiting. Red One was tasked with getting the pallets off the plane and stood by the forklift as the pilot dropped the back ramp.

"This isn't going to work," Earl said, looking into the back of the plane.

"What's not going to work?" Dan asked, walking out from the hangar.

"That forklift is too big to fit into the back," Earl said.

Mack, in classic fashion, said, "Can we use the forklift to pick up the front of the plane and have everything slide out the back?"

Dan, who would have usually been amused, was not. "Ok...

I wish I had an easier way, but we don't. So, let's get up there and do it by hand."

The team spent the next hour and a half unloading the cache by hand. Once they cleared a pallet, they would pass if off the back of the plane where it would be re-packed, re-banded, and placed on the truck by the forklift.

Mack and Evan walked down the ramp with the last box and set it on a pallet. Mack bent over and rested his hands on his knees. His tee-shirt was drenched in sweat as Dan walked up and knelt beside him.

"You ok cupcake?" Dan asked.

"I'm fine. Just taking a breather," Mack answered.

"How are your boys now?" Dan asked.

"Thawed, Dan," Mack replied.

"So, your boys aren't frozen anymore?" Dan said with fake concern.

"No. They thawed out nicely. Your concern means so much to me," Mack answered.

Dan laughed as he stood back up. "Alright, boys load up. We need to get to the embassy so we can get recon out the door."

***

The sun had gone down as the team started to work, going into their second night without sleep. Brian secured embassy vehicles to send out the recon teams, while the rest stayed behind to set up the BOO. The whole team worked together to set up the medical tent and then the command tent. Afterward, each squad would set up their individual tents.

In the command tent, Brian was having trouble getting a signal on his SAT phone. "Is this thing broken?"

Wes Rodgers, who was the teams' Communications Specialist (com spec), was busy setting up the tactical communications. "Uh...Chief, if you walk outside of the tent and away from the buildings, the satellites will see you better," Wes advised.

"Oh. Yeah, I guess that makes sense," Brian said.

Brian walked out of the command tent into the large courtyard of the embassy. About sixty seconds later, the signal strength on the sat phone was full. *Hmm, never doubt the propeller heads,* he thought to himself.

Karen answered the phone in the ops center back in Virginia.

"Chief, how are you guys doing over there?"

"We are fine. We are getting the BOO finished, and we have both recon teams out doing assessments with tech search. Karen, I don't have long to talk, is Kevin nearby?"

"Yeah, he's right here."

"Thanks"

"Hey Brian, its Kevin. What's your SIT REP?"

"We were able to get a good look at the damage when we flew in, and it's worse than we thought. Did you finish the roster for another team?"

"Most of it. We have a few holes. Still need a couple of med specs," Kevin said.

"Ok. You need to find a way to plug those holes because we will need them down here ASAP."

"Copy that, Brian. We will steal and pillage what we need for the second cache and get them alerted as soon as I get off the phone."

"Thanks, Chief"

"Hey Brian, you guys be careful down there. We hear reports about some big aftershocks."

"Yeah. We have felt a few good ones already. Listen, I need to get going. I'll check back in later when the squads start moving out."

"Ok, Brian. Be safe."

He disconnected the sat phone and returned to the command tent. As he entered, he saw Riley sitting at the mobile radio.

"Ok, copy that Red Recon. Stand by there while we get a squad on the way."

Riley turned to see that Brian had returned.

"Just talked to Red Recon, who is at the Hotel Montana. They have a lot of shout outs but are having trouble pinpointing them. They said the whole building is pancaked, but the good news is they have a lot of void spaces where there might be some survivors and good access for the squads."

"Ok, Riley. Who is up first?" Brian asked.

"Red Squad One," Riley answered.

"Let's get them moving," Brian advised.

"Roger that," Riley answered.

Riley jumped up and headed out of the command tent. Walking across the embassy compound, he saw Red One setting up their tent next to the medical tent.

"Hey Dan, got a second?" Riley called out.

"Yeah, give me a few." Dan finished pinning one of the aluminum uprights that supported the roof of the tent and walked over to meet Riley.

"What's up, Riley?" Dan asked.

"Red One is up first. We are sending you to the Hotel Montana. It has heavy damage with the potential for a lot of victims."

"Ok. Did the second half of the cache get here, because we are going to need our generator, and..."

Riley interrupted Dan. "It's here. Logistics is loading up

a stake body truck right now with generator, lights, breakers, chippers, and hand tools. Oh, and tell Doug the medical site box is on there as well."

Dan nodded. "Good."

"Keep your MREs and water close to you and don't eat or drink out in the open. And keep your fuel for the generator nearby as well. These people are desperate and will take desperate measures, just as you or I would do if we were in their shoes," Riley said.

"I have to admit I really did not think about that," Dan replied.

"Leave the tent. I'll get another squad to finish for you. Get going," Riley said.

With that, Dan turned to the squad. "Red One, we're up first. Leave the tent and grab your packs."

HOTEL MONTANA

The Virginia Urban Search and Rescue Team's first deployment was to Soviet Armenia in 1988 to assist in rescue efforts following an earthquake. Since then, the team had deployed on forty domestic missions and twenty-three internationally, yet with all that operational experience, they soon realized Haiti was going to be altogether different.

The horizon in the east was just starting to change color as Red One slowly made their way through the streets. They rode in silence. Doug, Mack, and Earl stood on one side of the truck, while Evan and Dan stood on the other.

Doug watched as a man walked over to a body with a small plastic bowl and throw its contents onto it, strike a match, and set it on fire.

None of them could wrap their brains around what their eyes were telling them. From the other side of the truck, Dan and Evan watched as a family carried a body out to the curb, where they laid it down and placed a piece of cardboard over the top of it.

Red One eventually made their way to the Hotel

Montana. Several road closures and subsequent detours marked their trip. Many of the citizens made make-shift houses in the middle of the streets using cinder blocks from the rubble for walls and pieces of wood as roofs. By building them in the street, it kept them out of the collapse zones from other buildings nearby. They were not going back into any building that was heavy enough to kill them.

An eight-foot wall surrounded the Montana, where a guard stood with an automatic weapon.

"Uh, Dan... you sure we are in the right place?" Mack asked with his stare fixed on the man with the rifle.

"Yeah, we're in the right place. Stay cool," Dan answered.

The guard walked around and looked at what the squad had with them in the back of the truck. Dan could tell from his expression he was starting to put it together.

"You help? Help?" the guard said in broken English.

Dan emphatically nodded his head. "Yes! We help!"

The guard quickly turned to unlock what was a well-fortified gate. After the squad's truck pulled through, the guard gave them a big smile and a thumbs up. "Merci! Merci beaucoup!"

"They speak French here?" Mack asked.

"Yes," Evan answered, turning around to face the squad. "Actually, many of the Haitians speak Spanish,

French, and English. So be careful what you say and where you are saying it."

At the top of the hill, they reached the front of the hotel. The squad stared dumbfounded by the amount of damage, observing the floors collapsed on top of each other.

Mark Lucas, a tech search specialist and longtime member of the team, met the squad as they were unloading. "Hey, guys! Get any sleep?"

"Nope. We were still setting up the BOO when they sent us out," Dan said as he was shaking Mark's hand. "So, what do you have for us?"

"A big mess. Just about the whole building is pancaked. All the easy rescues have been made. We have been doing a lot of call-outs, and we marked where we had responses, but after doing several laps, the spots where we could hear someone calling out are now silent. So, either they went unconscious or worse," Mark said.

"Do you have a good starting point?" Dan asked, looking at the hotel.

"Yeah. Around back on side Charlie. It has a courtyard and a good place to store gear and equipment. You should be able to leave the generator on Bravo and run extension cords from there," Mark said.

First responders, specifically firefighters, used Alpha, Bravo, Charlie, and Delta to reference a specific side of a structure. Alpha being front, the left side was Bravo, the back Charlie, and the right side was Delta. Now and then they would use Charlie Foxtrot to describe an area where things were not quite going according to plan.

"Can we get any closer with the truck?" Dan asked.

"No. This is it. You're going to have to hump everything from here," Mark said.

"Ok, no worries. Guys, you heard him. Generator on Bravo and everything else around to Charlie," Dan said.

"Dan, I'll walk around with you. There is a problem back there that one of your guys is going to have to take care of first. Likely Doug," Mark said.

Dan stopped and turned around to face Mark. "What problem?" Dan asked.

***

Dan followed Mark around to an area on the other side of the hotel where a portion of the building had collapsed into a lean-to. Mark ducked underneath and crawled into a void space while Dan followed.

"Well, that is a problem," Dan said, staring at a body hanging upside down, with one leg pinned.

"Dan, through this opening, is where we heard one of the voices during our call outs," Mark said. "It was a female voice but couldn't make out what she was saying. If you can get him out of there, you should have room to get back in there to get a better idea of where she is."

Dan knelt beside the body studying how the concrete collapsed around it.

"Did you try to move it out?" Dan asked.

"Yeah, but his leg is pinned deep. It didn't move even a little bit. If it weren't for the need of quick egress, I would say leave him in place. But with all the..."

"Aftershocks," Dan finished for him.

"Yeah, those."

"We will take care of this," Dan finally said.

"Ok, Dan, we are out. They have another site they want us to recon. See you back at the BOO."

"Thanks, Mark. Stay safe," Dan said, still staring at the body hanging upside down.

The rest of the squad finished bringing up the gear and started staging it near the void space where Dan was.

"Earl, can you run a cord back to the generator and bring in the Sawzall?" Dan called out.

"Got it," Earl replied.

"Also, send Doug in here," Dan asked.

"Will do."

A few moments later, Dan heard Doug crawling in behind him.

"I guess that is the problem," Doug said dryly.

"We need to get him out of here, Doug," Dan said.

"Umm, sure. Do you want to use the chippers?"

"No. I don't like the way the concrete above us is resting on the piece we would be chipping. It could shift on us."

"What about a Georgia haul?" Doug asked.

A Georgia haul was a technical term for getting your biggest guys to pull, push, pry, leverage, or otherwise move something that was in the way.

"No. Recon tried. Didn't work," Dan answered.

"I guess we could try and..." Doug was not able to finish his thought before he was interrupted by Earl, who crawled in with a Sawzall connected to an extension cord.

"Here, Dan," Earl said.

"Thanks, Earl," Dan said, taking the tool and placing it between himself and Doug.

Doug looked at what Earl had carried into Dan then back at the body, and the impending scenario started to take form.

"Dan, is your plan for me to take his leg off with a Sawzall?" Doug asked.

"You have a better idea, Doug?"

"Yeah, I do. I just haven't thought of it yet," Doug replied.

"Doug, we need to get in there, but he needs to be out of there first."

"Dan, I get it. But on my way back here, I passed two camera crews. They could be CNN for all we know."

"And?" Dan asked.

"And... I can't fire up a Sawzall and walk out with three-quarters of person forty-five seconds later."

Their dialogue started to escalate when they both turned to see Dr. Bruce crawling up to where they were.

Doug was relieved to see him. "Hey, Doc. We have a little problem here."

"You sure do," he said as he made a quick assessment of the body. "Dan, Doug and I got this. Do me a favor and get us the football. We won't be using that saw."

The "football" was the code word for the amputation kit.

"Doug, I agree with you. We need to give dignity whenever we can, but we are going to take his leg off," Bruce said.

Doug knew as much; he just wasn't sure what Bruce's plan was.

"I know we only talked about this one, but you are going to dis-articulate the right hip. Do you remember your landmarks for that?" Dr. Bruce asked.

Doug nodded as he started to cut the pants off the body. "Yep, I'm good."

While Doug prepped the body for the amputation, Evan crawled back, carrying the football.

"Thanks, Evan," Doug said. "Do you mind hanging out while I get this done? After I get through his ligament, I will need your help lowering him down."

"Of course. Just let me know when and what you want me to do."

Doug opened the football and pulled out two scalpels.

After putting on medical exam gloves and safety glasses, he moved into position. Doug made a long incision going from the medial side lateral to the outside of the leg and underneath as far as he could reach before the concrete stopped him. He kept making the same cut repeatedly, slicing deeper into the tissue and muscle.

"Evan, I don't have enough room to get the scalpel all the way through. I need you to roll his upper body your way as much as you can," Doug instructed.

Evan reached up and grabbed the body with both his arms and rolled him as much as he could.

Doug started cutting again. His hand disappeared into the body as he attempted to make the cuts through to the other side of the leg.

"Ok, Evan, I'm through. I need to reposition to cut the ligament, and he will drop when I do," Doug said.

"Copy. I'm ready."

Twenty minutes later, after he made the first incision, the body dropped into Evan's arms, and he and Dr. Bruce carefully lowered him to the ground.

Having nothing else to cover the body with, Doug grabbed a shower curtain out of the rubble.

"Doug, you're good at what you do," Evan said as they finished wrapping the body.

"Thanks, buddy."

Earl and Mack crawled in and dragged the body out, then placed it in the corner of the courtyard.

"Earl, Mack, I need you to crawl in and make some call outs," Dan said, looking down at the body in the shower curtain. "Let's see if we can get a better idea of where that female voice is located."

As they made their way into the small opening, they could see there was another larger opening further back into the building that led to an ample void space. Once they made it to the void space, Earl started calling out.

"HELLO! CAN ANYONE HEAR ME? HELLO!"

They sat in silence, listening. Above their head was a busted PVC pipe that extended into the debris and out toward the front side of the building.

Earl and Mack looked at each other. "Did you hear that?" Mack asked, looking at the pipe.

"Yeah. It sounds like it's coming from the front."

Mack called out again and asked where they were, but could not make out what they were saying.

They made their way back out of the building to the courtyard, where they saw Dan talking to a Haitian male.

"Dan, we just heard a voice coming out of a pipe, but we can't make out what they said. It looks like it's extending from the alpha side," Earl said, pointing to where the pipe was.

"Alright, this is starting to make sense now. Guys, this is John. He is here looking for his uncle, who is a bartender. He said he just heard a voice coming out of a pipe on the front side," Dan said.

John looked inquisitively at the Earl and Mack. "Do you think this could be the same voice you heard?"

Earl nodded his head. "It might be."

RITE OF PASSAGE

Heather was nervous. She was slated for the next recon mission with her Belgian Malinois Shepard, Thor, and wondered what she had gotten herself into. So rather than sitting and letting her mind cloud with negative energy, she decided that she and Thor needed a walk across the embassy compound.

"C'mon Thor, let's get some fresh air."

She made her way over to the command board to see where squads and recon teams were and wondered what they were doing.

Brian walked up from behind her. "Hey, Heather. You all set to go?"

"You're sending me out? Where am I going?" Heather asked.

Brian smiled. "Easy. You are not going out right now. It was just a general question."

"Sorry, Brian. I'm nervous. I want to fit in, and I don't want to let anyone down."

"I know it can be hard as a civilian trying to fit in here, but the best advice I can give you is just to be yourself and don't try too hard. Just let the process happen naturally," Brian said.

Heather nodded. "Ok."

"Are the guys messing with you?" Brian asked.

"Like being mean to me?"

"No. Are they teasing or hazing you?" Brian said, explaining what he meant.

"Oh, yeah. They are. I just figured it was a rite of passage kind of deal," Heather said.

"Well, that's part of it, but when they stop messing with you, that's when you know there is a problem. It's their way of letting you know they like you or not."

Heather smiled. "Thanks, Chief, I appreciate it."

"Please, call me, Brian. Out here, rank doesn't matter. It's about getting the job done. I am surrounded by personnel that are not officers who know this job better than I ever will. Stay humble and listen. It will take you a long way with these guys."

Riley walked out of the command tent and saw the two of them standing there.

"There you are. I just got off the phone with the engineers. They are having conniptions about where some of the squads are working. They're worried about the structural integrity and aftershocks," Riley said.

"Riley, do they have a choice? We have no cribbing," Brian said.

"I'm on your side Brian, but you need to talk to the engineers."

"I'll handle it," Brian said, rubbing his forehead.

"Heather, how are you doing? Ready to go out?" Riley asked, turning toward her.

"Yeah, we were just talking about that."

"Well, trust your technical search guys, and ask questions if you are not sure about something. You'll be fine."

"Thanks, Riley."

"You bet. Alright, I have to go take care of a code brown. Brian, I fill you on the rest when I get back," Riley said, walking away.

Heather did a double-take as Riley turned to walk away.

"Is that something I should know about, a code brown?" she asked.

Brian laughed. "No. That is his way of saying he has to go poop."

Heather dropped her head with an embarrassed smile.

"Right of passage, so to speak," Brian said as he gave her a friendly pat on the shoulder.

Heather's smile turned into a laugh.

***

Red One followed John back around to the Alpha side of the hotel to show them where he heard the voice. That area of the building had collapsed in a similar lean-to fashion; only it gave the team more room to work.

Evan crawled into space where broken pipes were extending out of the dirt from under the building. Evan held up his right arm with a closed fist.

"All quiet."

All quiet meant just that. Don't make a freaking sound. It was a term typically used with the tech search specialists when they used a listening device known as a Delsar. The Delsar was extremely sensitive and could pick up the sound of a mouse pissing on a cotton ball.

Evan was doing a call out and wanted to be able to hear any noise or voice traveling through the busted pipes.

"HELLO! CAN ANYONE HEAR ME?" Evan called out.

Nothing.

"HELLO! CAN ANYONE HEAR ME?" he repeated.

"I'm here! Here!

"That sounds a lot closer than where we were in the back," Earl said.

"What is your name?" Evan asked.

"Claudette. My name is Claudette."

"Claudette, my name is Evan. Can you tell me where you are in the building?"

"I was in the bar when the hotel collapsed."

That captured John's attention. "My uncle, is my uncle with her? His name is Samuel."

"Claudette is Samuel with you? Do you hear anyone else moving or talking around you?

"I can't see anything. It's too dark, but I was with Samuel when the floor collapsed on us."

"Claudette, can you call out for Samuel? Can you do that for us?" Evan asked as he turned to look at John.

Claudette called out for Samuel, but no answer.

"John, that doesn't mean anything. He could be unconscious," Dan said. "I'm not trying to give you false hope, but we won't know anything until we do, okay?"

John nodded.

"Guys, go back and get our gear. Let's leave the generator where it is and run cords from there," Dan said.

Earl, Doug, and Mack moved with purpose as Evan turned back toward the pipe.

"Claudette, we are going to start working our way back to you. You are going to hear a lot of noise out there. Ok?" Evan told her.

"Ok," Claudette answered.

Evan paused for a second, looking at the condition of the building, observing how all the pieces were resting on top of each other. *This would be easier if she were on the top floor,* he thought to himself. But as it was, they would have to tunnel underneath the weight of seven collapsed floors above them.

"Claudette, I need you to listen very carefully to me. It is going to take a while to get back to you. But we will not leave you alone. Someone will always be here, ok?"

"Ok. Thank you. Thank you for helping me," Claudette responded before she started crying.

"We need to be careful with our vibrations, so let's start with the chipper. Guys, remember, we need to be careful with what we cut and what we break. If we are not careful, someone will be coming to get us out of here," Evan said.

The chipper was a handheld jackhammer that could use different bits based on what needed to be busted or removed. The good news for Red One was the quality of the concrete was very poor. That made for easy tunneling. The bad news was that it wasn't strong, making it easier to collapse while trying to reach Claudette.

CLAUSTROPHOBIC NORWEGIAN

The sun had gone down again as Mack finished setting up lights at the entrance of the tunnel. The squad was making good progress.

The tunnel had only a twenty-four-inch diameter. Doug, being the biggest of them, had to use a lot of elbows and toes to squirm his way down when it was his turn to use the chipper. He was the living definition of a square peg in a round hole.

About thirty feet in, they reached a point where they started to go vertical, and there was no easy way to do it. Lying on their backs, they would chip away, clean their faces, then repeat.

Mack was on the chipper when he hit something solid.

"Hey Dan, I think I hit a metal shelf or something," Mack said, shouting so he could be heard at the other end of the tunnel.

"Ok. Do you think a Sawzall with a metal blade will work?" Dan asked.

"Yeah, it should."

"Alright, crawl out of there. I'm going to send Earl in."

"Copy," Mack replied.

Mack worked his way out of the tunnel, dragging the chipper behind him. Earl switched the cord over to the Sawzall and crawled his way back into where Mack had left off.

"Hey Doug, when Earl gets finished cutting, and if there is enough room, I want you to get in there to see if you can get back to Claudette," Dan said as he was looking down the tunnel at Earl.

"Will do. Let me get my hole bag ready," Doug said.

Many of the med specs had what they called a hole bag. It was a smaller bag they kept in their larger medical pack with enough to do a quick assessment, start an IV, and give drugs. Doug's main concern for Claudette was rhabdomyolysis, commonly referred to as crush syndrome.

This syndrome was caused by direct or indirect muscle injury and resulted from the death of muscle fiber, releasing their contents into the bloodstream.

Potassium and myoglobin were Doug's biggest fear factors. Once the pressure was released, or a heavy object, such as a large piece of concrete was lifted off a body part, potassium could make its way to the heart and cause lethal cardiac rhythms. Myoglobin, on the other hand, is a large protein that could cause renal failure.

To counteract the possible effects of the two, Doug would want to give D50 (IV glucose). This would cause an insulin release to carry sugar into the cells, and more importantly, take potassium along for the ride as well. Albuterol nebulizers also could remove potassium from the blood. As for the myoglobin, IV fluids alone would help dilute the concentration and hopefully allow the kidneys to flush them out before they could cause long term damage.

The sound of cutting metal stopped, and Earl could be heard down the tunnel muttering to himself as if he were Yosemite Sam. Claudette likely learned a few new words during his rant.

"Earl, what's up?" Dan yelled down the tunnel.

"I can't get this piece of metal out of here. It's cut all the way through, but it keeps binding on something on the other side."

The squad then heard what sounded like a tool striking a metal plate and something hitting the ground. The guys all just stared at each other.

"Earl, what was that?" Mack asked.

"I used the butt of the Sawzall to bust this damn thing out of the way," Earl called back down the tunnel. "We're good."

The rest of the squad just chuckled because they all had a picture in their head of what was going on in the tunnel. Earl was likely pissed off and tired of being outsmarted by an inanimate object and beat it into submission with the only tool he had, but it worked. Rescue techs had to innovate, not only using a tool for what it was initially designed for but what it could potentially do.

Earl worked his back out of the tunnel and slung the menacing piece of metal off to the side.

"Doug, you are clear for about four or five feet vertically. The cuts left some pretty sharp edges on the metal whatever it is, so watch out for that as you make your turn from horizontal to upright," Earl explained.

"Copy that," Doug replied.

"Hey, Evan, toss me my bag there," Doug asked as he moved toward the opening of the tunnel.

"Doug, you sure you don't want to get a running start?" Mack teased as Doug was wedging himself into the tunnel. Doug used the toe of his boot to kick dirt back on Mack.

The light on his helmet was able to penetrate the dust where he could see the end of the tunnel. When he reached the end, he craned his neck up to see the opening that was made. The only way he would make it up through the hole would be to roll over on his back and extend his arms to pull himself up.

He started to roll over to get into position when an

aftershock hit. He tried to protect himself, but there was nothing he could do but put his arms over his head as the Montana shook.

Outside the tunnel, Dan had a panicked look on his face. "Get the hell out of here," he yelled at the rest of the squad.

Both Dan and Evan dove for the opening of the tunnel to see if they could reach Doug and drag him out, but he was too far down to reach.

Doug yelled as debris was dropping down and bouncing off his helmet and arms.

Then as quickly as it started, the aftershock stopped.

"Doug...! Doug...! Are you alright?" Dan yelled down the tunnel.

Doug tried to answer between coughs. "I'm good. Just...just give me a few here."

Dan knew what that meant. Doug was shaken by what had just happened and needed a few moments to reset.

Doug was scared, but he had a right to be. He was wedged into an unprotected tunnel dug by hand, under tons of unstable concrete. The fact he was claustrophobic did not help either. The others knew confined space ops was not his favorite thing to do, but Doug never let on just how much it really did bother him.

Although Doug's specialty on the team was a medical

specialist, he was also qualified in technical rescue. The confined space portion of technical rescue school took place at the fire academy, where they had a series of reinforced concrete tunnels that ran in different directions connected by large vaults. And just to add to the enjoyment, it was all buried underground. As for the pipes, they varied in sizes from forty-eight inches in diameter down to twenty-four.

When it came time for the practical evolution for the final training rescue test, Doug had been paired with the only person bigger than him. Doug was 6'4" and 240 pounds and had big Norwegian shoulders genetically gifted to him by his father. His team partner was 6'5" and weighed in at a healthy 285 pounds. It had all the makings of an episode of Wild Kingdom with live footage of a giant python digesting two large wildebeests.

It had been raining most of the morning on the day of the final test, so naturally, water and mud had settled into the bottom of the 100-foot 24-inch diameter tunnel they had to crawl through and return in. It was difficult enough for the mammoth moles in the dry three-foot-wide tunnels, but with water and mud in the twenty-four-inch tunnels, it was just unfair.

To overcome this, Doug's partner entered the tunnel feet first, and Doug went in headfirst as they locked arms and inch wormed off each other's weight. One thing Doug knew is that no one would come between him and the exit of the tunnel, at least until they got to the other end.

Ultimately, what kept Doug from becoming totally

derailed and a human jackhammer was the fact his partner was more freaked out than he was. This took the focus off his own fear so he could concentrate on keeping his partner from doing what he himself was on the verge of doing. Perhaps this is what the sadistic instructors had in mind with this pairing from the start.

Doug slowly moved his arms back off his head so he could brush the rubble off that had fallen during the aftershock. As the air started to clear, he could see up through the hole. "Claudette! I forgot all about Claudette."

"Claudette! Can you hear me?" Doug shouted up the hole.

"Yes. I hear you."

Doug blew out a long breath.

"Doug, I think I can move now. Things shifted in here and..."

"Please don't move," Doug interrupted. "I can't imagine how tough it is to be where you are right now and how badly you want to move, but please stay still. I need to give you medicine before you start moving. Do you understand me, Claudette?"

Doug waited, staring into the darkness for her answer, but he heard nothing.

"Claudette, do you understand what I am telling you?"

"Yes, I understand," she replied.

Doug squirmed in the tunnel so he could get in a better

position to make the vertical ninety-degree turn from where he was lying face up. The light from his helmet focused through the hole above him, where he could see some sort of stainless-steel railing that looked strong enough to pull himself up.

He grabbed it with his left hand and started to pull while at the same time digging in with his heels to propel him forward and up. Doug was now standing.

There was still a lot of dust lingering in the air from the last aftershock, and it was difficult for him to make out his surroundings.

"I can see you! I see your light!"

Her voice was coming from behind Doug. As he turned to look toward Claudette, he was startled by a lifeless face directly in front of him.

Claudette could see the silhouette of Samuel cast by Doug's light.

"Is that Samuel? Is he ok?"

Doug looked down at the body's chest, where he saw a name tag. It was Samuel.

In an emotionless response, Doug said, "Yes, it's Samuel."

"Is he...?"

"I'm sorry, Claudette."

Doug was an experienced field medic and had been on

several scenes where he had to tell a family member or a friend that a person was dead. It was important to use the word dead as not to give any ambiguity or false hope in situations like that. This time it was not needed.

Claudette wept.

Doug's focus returned to getting her out. It didn't take him long to determine that Samuel was going to have to be moved for that to happen. The problem was that his upper torso and right arm were heavily entangled.

"Claudette, I need to go out for just a couple of minutes to get some tools and other things we will need to get you out. I will only be gone for a short time, ok?"

She sniffled and said, "Well, it's not like I am going anywhere."

Doug chuckled. "You know, with a sense of humor like that, we might have a job for you."

Moments later, Doug crawled back out of the tunnel. He took his helmet off and wiped debris from his face.

"You good?" Dan asked.

"Yeah, just scared me."

"We all were Doug," Dan said. "What do we have up there?"

"We have room to work, but just enough. And uh..." Doug paused.

"What?" Dan asked with concern.

Doug stopped to look around to see who was in earshot of where they were. "Where's John?"

"He went down to grab some MREs. What's up?"

"I found Samuel. He's dead. But it gets worse. His upper body is entangled and blocking the only access we have to Claudette," Doug explained.

Dan shifted his stare from Doug down the dark tunnel as he processed what he heard.

"When you say entangled, how entangled are we talking about?"

"Well, I think we will have to do this your way Dan," Doug answered.

"Well, Doug, not that you really need any type of consolation at this point, but you were right," Dan said, smacking him on the knee.

"I was right about what?" Doug asked.

"We got a call from the BOO not long after the shock hit to check on us," Dan said.

"I'm not tracking you, Dan?" Doug said tiredly and with a tinge of annoyance.

"They told us there was footage all over the states now with you doing that amputation. It was CNN."

"WE HAVE COTS..."

As the squad approached the lighted site where work was being done, they saw two sets of legs that stuck out from a tunnel that extended underneath the building. Ron walked up and kicked the boots that were sticking out the furthest.

"Hey, you going to do anything today?" Ron asked.

Doug crawled out and looked up at Ron. With dirt and sweat all over his face, Doug managed to give him a small grin.

"Man, they weren't kidding, you guys look spent. Heard you had to use the football this morning. Did you use a tourniquet?" Ron joked.

"Actually, I didn't," Doug said with a smirk.

Doug tapped Dan's leg to back out. "Blue squad is here."

"We heard they were sending another squad to help out," Doug said as he stood up with a groan.

"We are not here to help you; we are here to replace you."

"What?" Dan and Doug said in unison.

"Red One has been up for over seventy-two hours. You guys haven't slept since the night before we deployed. Your chauffeur awaits down by the gate. Leave everything where it is. We got it. Just bring your packs," Ron explained.

Red One didn't like it, but they weren't going to fight it either.

"Ok, Doug, give Ron a heads up about what we have here and what he is going to have to do," Dan said as he turned to go find the Blue squad leader.

"What the heck is he talking about, Doug?" Ron asked with wide eyes.

"I'm not the only one who will be doing an amputation today, Ron," Doug said to Ron raising his eyebrows.

"Ok, you have my attention now," Ron said.

"You have a deceased victim that is blocking both access and egress to a live one. His name is Samuel. He is the uncle of John, who is a local that has been helping us out today. From what I understand, Doc M. is here and has already explained everything to him. John has given his blessing to do whatever it is we need to do to save her."

Ron let out a soft whistle.

"Right. Ron, listen, your live victim's name is Claudette. She is hanging tough, but I fear once you guys get her into a position that you can extricate her, she is going go full crush syndrome on you, so make sure you preload her before any movement."

Ron nodded his head. "Copy."

"Did you bring a medical site box with you?" Doug asked.

"Yeah, they are bringing it up now," Ron replied.

"Good deal. I'm going to bring ours back for rehab and restock," said Doug. "Ron, listen, I think this is going to be easiest just to use the Sawzall. It's dark in there, and if done right, Claudette will not know what it is you are cutting."

"Got it," Ron said, in a half convincing voice.

Doug felt bad for dumping such a heavy load on Ron, but it was now his watch. "You need me to do anything before I roll out," Doug asked.

"Nope, all good here," Ron answered.

Doug gave him a pat on the back and turned to walk down to the gate.

"Hey Doug, you and the boys did a heck of a job here today," Ron said.

"Thanks, bro. Good luck," Doug called over his shoulder.

***

The backup alarm could be heard as Red Squad One was

backing into the embassy compound. To a man, they were dirty, tired, and moving slow. Brian, Mike, and Riley came out to meet them as they were unloading.

"Good work out there, Dan," Brian said as Dan was getting his pack off the back of the truck.

"It was them that did all the work," Dan said as he watched his squad walk wearily toward the tents.

"How's Doug" Brian asked.

"He's fine. He got a little scare with the aftershock, but then again, we all did," Dan answered.

Brian paused before he spoke again. "This probably isn't what you want to hear, but we only have a small window for you guys to get rested up. We need to send you up north of here to University. It was heavily occupied at the time of the quake with a lot of damage."

Dan nodded.

"Logistics will rehab your gear," Riley added. "You guys go ahead and bed down and leave me your sat phone, and I will get it charged up for you."

Dan took it out of his pack and tossed it to Riley.

"Thank you, sir," said Dan.

The rest of the team was already heading for the tents. Mack stopped at the portable sink, using both hands to give himself a mini shower. The water felt nice and cool as he splashed it in his face and all around his neck. He dug into his pack, where he pulled a small towel that was carefully folded into a zip lock bag and dried his face and hands. Afterward, Mack positioned his pack on the ground and used it as a pillow.

Evan saw him lying there as he headed for the tents. "Hey, you know we have cots over here?"

"Yeah, I know. I just want to watch the stars for a little bit," Mack answered.

"Suit yourself," Evan said without looking back.

Mack lay motionless as everything around him became increasingly quieter. The stars even seemed to be dwindling as their light started to fade.

That was odd, Mack thought to himself as the stars seemed to light back up. And then suddenly, it was doing it again – fading, fading, darker, darker, darker still, and then out.

***

Riley entered Red Squad One's tent with a flashlight, finding his way over to Dan's cot, where he tapped Dan on the shoulder.

"Dan, sorry, bro, but time to get up. Brian wants to see you in the command tent," Riley nudged.

"What's wrong with my tent?" Dan grumbled.

Dan managed to force himself out of his cot and outside, where he met up with Riley. As they were walking over to the command tent, Riley noticed Mack lying on the ground by the sink.

"Is he alright?" Riley asked.

Dan had no idea what Riley was talking about until he followed his stare to where Mack was sprawled across the ground as if dropped out of the sky.

"I'm sure he is fine. Just leave him alone," instructed Dan.

As they were walking toward the command tent, Brian was coming out and walked over to meet Dan and Riley.

"Dan, sorry for the short sleep time, but we need to get you guys up and moving toward University. They found a hole where there are two or three females and have voice contact with one of them. We are not certain how..." Brian was distracted.

"Is he ok?" Brian asked, looking over at Mack.

"Damn it, he's fine. He's just sleeping," Dan replied with an edge.

"We have cots, you know," Brian said, still looking at Mack.

"Well, he didn't get that far. Now, are you going to finish telling me what the hell we got, or do you want me just to figure it out when I get there?" Dan snapped back.

By department standards, Dan was a Captain, and Brian was a Chief, and this was one of those moments where rank didn't matter, and Brian was aware of it. He had someone who had been up for over seventy-two hours with only three hours rest and really didn't care about one of his squad members sleeping on the ground.

"Uh, sure, Dan," Brian said, starting over. "We are not certain how deep this void space is, so we are sending some extra gear if you have to set up a haul system."

"Ok, copy that," Dan said.

"It's going to be a hot one today as well, so be sure to bring an extra couple of cases of water along," Riley added.

"Here's your sat phone too. She is all charged up for you, along with an extra battery. I don't expect you will be able to reach us on the portables today."

"Got it. Thanks, Riley."

After the briefing, Dan walked over to Mack and stood over top of him. He could see his chest was moving up and down, which provided some comfort to the squad leader.

"Mack, time to get up," Dan ordered.

Nothing.

"Mack, c'mon, we have to get moving," he cajoled.

Nothing. Dan kicked him. Still nothing. Dan got a half panicked look on his face as Evan walked up beside him with his pack on.

"He alright?" Evan asked.

"We are about to find out," Dan said. "Got an extra bottle of water I can borrow?"

"Here," Evan said, passing Dan the water.

Dan opened the water and sprayed it all over Mack's face. "Ah, you are alive," Dan mused as Mack was choking on the water that made its way into his nose.

Dan and Evan had already turned to walk away. "Get up, or you're going to miss the bus," Dan yelled back.

"Bus?" Mack said as he flopped back down onto his pack. I don't even know where my lunch box and crayons are."

UNIVERSITY

The squad had a quiet ride to the university, mainly because Mack was fast asleep. The others watched as they drove past more carnage. They felt like there was no end to it.

Evan remained motionless except for his eyes moving from one disturbing sight to another.

"I shouldn't be used to seeing this for being here so short of time," he said softly, still staring out of the back of the truck.

"Evan," Doug said, "I was just thinking that very thing."

Evan looked at Doug.

"It doesn't make us heartless; it just allows us to do what it is we came here to do Evan," Doug said

Other than being responsible for the medical 911 of his squad, Doug kept an eye on the psychological status as well. So far, no one had the 1,000-yard stare, and Doug didn't really expect he would see it either, at least not from anyone on his squad.

Dan was staring down at his hand-held GPS.

"We are about 15 minutes out. Evan and I will do a walk around while the rest of you bring the gear up."

The rest of the squad acknowledged Dan. "Copy."

Doug started rifling through his pack to make sure he had things the way he wanted them. Then he put a couple of creature comforts into his leg bag for the squad–things like moleskin for blisters and such, and Advil.

When he placed the Advil into his leg bag, the squad could hear the pills shifting around. It didn't take long before he realized the whole squad was staring at him like a pack of Pavlovian dogs. It even woke Mack up.

"What?" Doug said, looking back at them.

"Is that prescription strength?" Mack asked, staring at Doug's leg bag.

"It is if I give you four of them," Doug quipped.

Mack waved his hand at him, motioning him to pass them over.

Mack took four and passed them to Earl, who took four and then passed them to Evan, who took four and passed them to Dan. Dan paused and looked at everyone else.

"Oh well, when in Haiti…" Dan's voice trailed off.

"I'm on a squad with a bunch of junkies," Doug said under his breath.

They all laughed as Dan tossed the bottle back to Doug, who shook it to see if there were any left.

"C'mon Doug," Mack said. "We all know you carry the good stuff, and you're holding it for yourself."

"Well, Mack," Doug said as he was packing the rest of his gear away, "If you manage to sever an appendage, I promise I will give you some more Advil."

"Advil?" Mack questioned.

"Yeah, Advil! You glue sniffer," Doug teased.

The morning air was becoming warm and thick as the squad was backing their truck into the university. Dan and Evan set off to recon the site as Earl, Mack, and Doug unloaded the gear.

The slight breeze there was shifted as they finished staging their gear when each of them came to an immediate standstill.

"What was that?" Mack asked as he held his hand up over his nose.

Earl motioned with his head. "Pretty sure it's coming from over there."

Doug and Mack turned to see piles of bodies being stacked up against the wall that ran behind the school. They were lined up in rows of approximately twenty each and stacked four high with nothing to protect them from the hot, humid air.

"I feel like I'm living in a WWII documentary," Doug said with an unbelieving look on his face.

"Well, at least we are not being shot at," Earl replied in an attempt to add something positive to a very grim moment.

Doug's attention shifted from the piles of bodies to the collapsed school, and he couldn't help but wonder what awaited him.

The three started to put on their half-mask respirators to help filter out the smell of decaying bodies as Dan and Evan reached the top of the collapsed school. A Haitian male saw them from a distance and started to yell and wave at them.

"Rescue! Rescue!" he said to Dan and Evan.

Next to him was a middle-aged Haitian female who was on her knees, peering down into the building. She jumped up to her feet when she heard those words being yelled and ran over to Dan and Evan.

"Thank you! Thank you so much for coming," she said as she gave them both hugs while tears rolled down her face.

"My name is Liezel; we think my daughter Nadine is over here," she said as she pulled at them to follow her.

The Haitian male approached them as Liezel was directing Evan and Dan.

"I am Nelson. I can show you where I talked to one of the girls. Nadine was with them when the quake hit."

Dan nodded calmly. "Ok, listen, Liezel, I need you to go back down off the building. It's not safe to be up here. If we get another aftershock, everything could shift, and you could get seriously hurt. Nelson will take us over to where he talked to Nadine's friend, and then he will join you down there, ok?"

"I understand. Please save my Nadine. She is all I have," Liezel said.

"I promise we will do everything we possibly can," Dan said, reassuring her.

They followed Nelson higher up to the spot where he was able to talk Nadine's friend Stephanie.

"Does Stephanie speak English?" Evan asked Nelson as he looked down into the hole with his light.

"Yes. They all do, according to Liezel," Dan responded.

"Good...that's good," Evan replied.

"Listen, Nelson; I have a big job for you. I need you to keep an eye on Liezel for me. We need to keep her encouraged without giving her false hopes. Does that make sense?"

"Yes, keep her from expecting the worse until we know more," Nelson answered.

"I couldn't have said it better. And what you did here was great work, Nelson. It saved us a lot of time," Dan said.

Dan walked back over to Evan, who was still looking down into the building when he started to call out.

"Stephanie! Stephanie, can you hear me?" Evan called out.

Silence.

"Stephanie! Stephanie!" Evan called again.

Evan could hear someone coughing. "Stephanie, is that you? Can you hear me?" Evan repeated.

"Yes, I can hear you," Stephanie said.

"Good, Stephanie, good. My name is Evan. We are getting ready to come down there and get you out. We need you to stay calm and try to stay awake so we can talk to you, ok."

"Ok, I'll try. I'm very tired," she answered back.

"I understand," Evan replied.

"Are you injured or just trapped?" Evan asked from above, trying to see down into the dark cavern.

"I think my left leg is broken, but I can't feel it anymore," Stephanie faintly replied.

"Ok, Stephanie. We have a medic who is going to take good care of you. Can you see any other students around you?" Evan questioned.

"I can see Nadine, but she isn't talking or moving. And Mary, I can't see where she is. She left to go downstairs right before the building started shaking," Stephanie spoke, her voice wavering.

"Alright. We are going to check on her too. We will be down soon to help both of you, ok?" Evan said, trying to give her what comfort he could.

"Thank you, Evan. Thank you so much."

Evan continued to study how the collapsed floors were positioned. He couldn't make sense of how they collapsed the way they did or why they were still standing the way they were. His main concern was stability, and it was a concern that left as quickly as it came. There was nothing he could do about it anyway. It was no different than the tunnel they were in the day prior.

Dan made his way back over to Evan, who was just standing up from the entrance to the hole.

"What do you think?" Dan asked.

"Definitely need a lowering system, but don't trust anything in this pile to use as an anchor," Evan said as he scanned the immediate area.

"What about our truck?" Dan suggested looking down. "That's pretty bombproof."

"Bombproof, maybe, but is it earthquake-proof?" Evan questioned.

"I think it's all we got, Evan," Dan replied.

Evan took his helmet off and scratched his head. "Copy."

"Go get it moved into position and have Mack harness up," instructed Dan. "I'll stay with Stephanie."

Evan turned and started heading down the pile. Dan scanned the area to find Doug. He spotted him down by the gate, looking inside the medical site box. Dan whistled at him and pointed at his radio and then made a circular motion with his hand in the air. Doug knew that meant to go to the talk around channel because they were too far away from the BOO to hit the repeater.

Dan could see Doug keying up his radio.

"Go," said Doug.

"Harness up. You're going in behind Mack after he does a recon to see what we need," instructed Dan.

"Copy," Doug affirmed

"Hey, Doug," Dan called over the radio

"Yep," Doug answered.

"Bring the bag with the good stuff too. I think they will need it before we start moving broken bones around," Dan said.

"Well, it's not like I have any Advil left anyway," Doug replied.

"ON-ROPE"

Evan crawled under the front of the truck that was now positioned in line with the school. He carried with him two pieces of two-inch webbing that he placed over the top of the axel and pulled the looped ends back out from under the truck.

If they pull the truck up the pile and down into the hole on top of them, we have much bigger problems to deal with, Evan thought as he finished connecting the anchor to the belay line.

Dan's radio chirped to life. "Dan, we are good down here. Just let me know when they are on the rope so we can do a quick load test before they go over the edge," Evan said.

"Copy," Dan replied as Mack was approaching the top of the pile.

Dan was holding the other end of the belay line with a figure-eight knot tied in it with a carabiner and handed it to Mack.

"On rope," Dan called down to Evan over the radio.

"On belay," Evan called back, indicating he was ready to either let line out or brake depending on what the call was for.

"You ready for a load test Mack," Dan asked.

"Yeah, let me move away from the hole," Mack replied.

"Pull slack out for load test," Dan called down to Evan.

Evan pulled the slack out so Mack could lean back with all his weight putting stress on the line to make sure it would hold.

Moving away from a hole or the edge of a long drop was always a good idea when doing a load test. Otherwise, sudden deceleration trauma would be the first indicator that there was a problem with the system.

Mack moved back over to the hole and positioned himself to be lowered.

"Good?" Dan asked one last time checking Mack's carabiner.

"Yeah, give me some slack," Mack responded.

Dan called down to Evan for slack, which allowed Mack to slowly back through the opening and fall backward in a controlled manner and speed, so only the tips of his boots were touching the edge. That allowed him to gently remove his feet when the time came to prevent the rope from bouncing off the edge, creating unnecessary friction.

"Lower," Mack called back up as he turned on his helmet

light to get a better look around. Less than a minute later, Mack touched down on the bottom.

"Slack," Mack yelled up to Dan so he could disconnect the carabiner from his harness.

Mack saw Stephanie off to the right. "Stephanie, my name is Mack, and we are going to get you out of here, ok? I just need to take a quick look around to see if there are others down here with you."

"Yes, ok. Thank you for coming to help us, Mack."

"You are welcome, Stephanie."

Taking a look around, Mack got a quick count of about eight that were beyond help. Moving his helmet up to look at the top of the hole, he saw another student that was obviously deceased hanging upside down and entangled in what appeared to be blinds from a window.

"Mack, can you check on Nadine? I need to know if she is ok," Stephanie pleaded.

"I sure can, Stephanie. I am heading there right now."

Nadine was lying face-up on a big piece of splintered concrete with another piece that was partially on top of her. The top piece was precariously cantilevered over her left side and looked like it was lying directly on her left shoulder and arm. The only thing that kept the top piece from completely crushing her was that the other side was barely being held up by a piece of rebar connected to another big chunk of concrete hanging from the floor above.

Mack carefully approached her by moving desks and other debris out of his way so he could get to her head. He noticed she had a large hematoma on her right forehead. He removed his rescue gloves and placed his fingers on her neck.

"She's alive," Mack whispered to himself.

He quickly made his way over to Stephanie. "I got some great news; Nadine is still alive." Stephanie started to cry.

"Ok, stay with me here. I need you to listen to me. We need to get her out first, ok?"

"Yes, please. Take care of Nadine. Oh, God, thank you, God," exclaimed Stephanie.

Mack gave her a soft pat on the arm. "I'm not going anywhere, but I need to tell the others what we need to get the two of you out, ok?"

"Yes, thank you so much."

"Dan! You there?" Mack yelled up to the top of the hole.

Dan poked his head in through the hole. "Yeah, what do you need?"

"I need Doug down here like now," Mack directed." Nadine is alive."

"What do you need to get her out?" Dan asked.

"Going to need some airbags to do lifts on both of them. But first, get Doug down here because he really needs to do some of his medic magic before we get started on either of them," Mack yelled back.

"Ok. He's standing right here. I'll pull the lineup and send him down; then Earl will come down with the cylinders and airbags," Dan said.

High-pressure airbags were commonly used in technical rescue and could be used to move weight as little as two tons and upwards of eighty tons. They literally could be used to lift a train off of someone. What made them ideal for search and rescue was that they were easily mobile and had low profiles for fitting into tight spots. Additionally, they could be operated with the same air cylinders they wore on their backs for structure firefighting.

The real difficulties were not so much if they had the capability of moving slabs of concrete, but rather what would happen when they did? Would it crumble under its own weight? Would its center of gravity shift when being lifted? Would it cause a secondary, or tertiary collapse because it was holding other large slabs in place above it, which were holding even more slabs in place? Courage without calculation could kill the whole squad along with the victims they were trying to rescue.

Mack turned to go back to Stephanie to get a better assessment of her situation when Dan yelled back down at him.

"Hey Mack, are you thinking about a vertical Stokes coming back out?" Dan asked.

"Uh sure Dan, but Doug will likely need to ride along with her. Do you have enough folks up there to help on the haul line?" Mack asked.

"I'll figure something out," Dan answered.

Mack laughed to himself. "Sounds like something Indiana Jones would say."

He made his way back over to Stephanie. "Ok, is there anything you can't move other than your left leg?" Mack asked.

"It's just my left leg," Stephanie answered.

"Does anything else hurt?" he asked.

"No," she replied.

"Do you have any medical problems we should know about before we move you out of here? Anything like diabetes or asthma?" Mack asked.

"No. Nothing I am aware of." Stephanie answered.

"Do you have any allergies to pain medications that you are aware of? The reason I ask that is that we will give you something to help with the pain before we move this concrete," Mack informed her.

"No. No allergies," Stephanie answered.

"Ok. That's good," Mack responded.

Doug touched down on the bottom the same time Mack finished asking Stephanie questions. He disconnected from the carabiner and yelled to Dan to pull it back up.

"I swear I will never make fun of another medic as long as I live," Mack said, walking over to Doug.

"Oh yeah, Mack boy?" Doug said with a smile. "No atheists in fox holes, huh?"

"No. I'm a believer," Mack said.

"Which one is Nadine?" Doug asked.

"She's over here on the left," Mack said, pointing.

Doug approached the site carefully as Mack did making his way over to her head. He took off his rescue gloves and put on medical exam gloves.

"Her level of consciousness makes sense with that big knot on her forehead," Doug said as he was shining his light down on her.

"Yeah, even I noticed that," Mack said.

"You really are quite the closet medic, aren't you Mack?" Doug joked.

"Uh, huh, that's me." Doug tried to open her eyes, and she resisted him as well. "Ok, that's a good sign. But still need to get a good look at her pupils." Doug firmly opened her eyes, and her pupils were still equal and reactive.

"Yeah, that's a real good sign," Doug said.

"Mack, do me a favor and get a blood pressure on her right arm. I don't care what her bottom number is, so don't worry about the stethoscope. Just need one over palp."

Doug took extra time to see how much of the concrete impinged on Nadine. From what he could tell, it was on her shoulder and the upper part of her arm. He was able to reach his hand underneath and check her radial pulse on her left wrist. It wasn't there.

Doug keyed up the radio, "Dan from Doug."

"Go, Doug," Dan answered.

"I'm going to need an oxygen bottle down here for an Albuterol neb, and the monitor from the site box. I'll need them in that order," Doug requested.

"Copy," Dan replied.

Mack had grabbed the cuff out of the bag and did as Doug asked.

"I think I'm getting something around ninety-ish," Mack advised.

"Ok. That's too low for pain meds right now. Let me get an IV in her, and maybe we can get it high enough to give them before we move her. What's the plan for moving this thing? It looks a little wonky."

"Earl is on his way down with airbags to do a lift. Hopefully, he has some idea of what to do about the top end hanging off that rebar. Hey, you want me to get a blood glucose while I'm over here?" Mack asked.

Doug shook his head. "Don't worry about it. We can just use the blood from the IV."

Doug repositioned himself over to Nadine's right arm. "Mack, I got a bottle of sterile water in my pack. Can you grab that so I can clean up her arm before I start this line?"

"Sure," Mack said, opening the pack. "Do you want the starter kit yet?"

"Yeah. Go ahead and pull that out and spike a liter for me and put it on a pressure bag," Doug requested.

Mack was not a medic, but he knew what Doug would want when he finished cleaning her arm. He opened up the IV pack all the way so it would unfold like a small suitcase. Next, he pulled out an elastic tourniquet and several alcohol preps and placed the whole kit up beside Doug on the concrete. Then, Mack pulled out a one-liter bag of normal saline IV fluid and inserted the spiked tip of the administration tubing, placing it into the pressure bag. IV fluids flow either by gravity or by pressure. In austere environments, such as collapsed buildings, IV poles were not readily available, so the med specs relied on pressure. It was a simple sleeve that the fluid bag could be inserted to with mesh on one side and a pressure cuff on the other. As fluids flowed out, it would periodically have to be pumped back up to increase for lost pressure.

"Just as I thought, a closet medic," Doug said as he picked

up the tourniquet and placed it tightly around Nadine's arm.

Mack smacked Doug on his helmet.

"Help a brother out with some extra light there, Mack," Doug asked as he started wiping down the forearm with alcohol preps looking for a vein.

"Aren't the veins bigger up by the elbow?" Mack asked.

"They are, but if I start high and miss, it will create a plumbing problem if I have to start one lower. So, I always start low unless I see one that Stevie Wonder couldn't miss," Doug said.

Mack nodded. "Makes sense. I doubt she would have one of those after being stuck under this thing for three days."

Doug gently flicked a vein he located on her arm, trying to get it to pop up. "I would like something bigger to get an 18-gauge in, but it looks like we will have to settle for a 20-gauge. We just need to push the D50 slow, so we don't blow her vein."

Mack handed him a 20 gauge IV as Doug pulled the skin tight on Nadine's arm to keep the vein from rolling as he attempted to thread the catheter into it.

Mack became distracted from above as he heard Earl calling to be lowered and turned to look up at him.

"Hey, ADD boy–light!" Doug reminded Mack.

"Oh, sorry, Doug. My bad."

Doug inserted the IV with confidence and waited for a flashback of blood in the catheter.

"Nice stick," Mack said as he handed him the IV tubing.

"Thanks. I got this. I know Earl will need help getting the airbags set up," Doug said.

Earl discontented the rope from the harness.

"Dan, I'm off the rope. Send the cylinders down," Earl requested.

Earl walked over to Mack with the high-pressure airbags and took a look under the concrete to see how much room he would have to make sure they get centered correctly.

"What are you thinking?" Mack asked.

"I think if we don't get this right, this slab will slide down on her," Earl said.

"You think?" Mack replied with a hint of sarcasm.

"Alright. I know that's obvious. What I mean is that if we can capture the weight somehow, other than what the airbags are lifting, we should be good," Earl said.

"We're going to need some rigging for that, though, aren't we?" Mack asked as he surveyed the upper part of the slab being held up by only the one piece of rebar.

Earl keyed up his radio. "Dan, can you call the BOO on the sat phone and get the twenty of heavy rigging?"

"Yeah. Standby," Dan replied over the radio.

"Are you thinking about a sling that we can girth hitch around the top part of the concrete?" Mack asked.

"That's exactly what I am thinking about," Earl replied.

"A few minutes later, Earl could hear Dan coming over his radio. "Earl, rigging is at the Montana right now, and they currently do not have any transportation to get down here."

"Copy," said Earl.

"Earl—from Evan, are you looking for something to sling the concrete with?"

Earl and Mack looked at each other. "I swear he is clairvoyant sometimes," Mack said, looking at Earl's radio.

"Yeah, Evan. That's exactly what we need. You got an idea?" Earl asked.

"Maybe," answered Evan. "We have a 30-foot cargo strap in the rear of the truck that could be used.

"Are we talking about one of those yellow industrial types?" Earl asked.

"Affirmative Earl," Evan said.

Earl looked at Mack. "I think we are in business, Mack."

Earl keyed up his radio again. "Dan, when you get a

chance, come back over to the hole so I can walk you through what we have in mind."

"Ok. Give me a few," Dan replied.

Earl turned around and looked at the concrete again with a pensive stare.

"Having second thoughts?" Mack asked.

"No. I just think that most of the contact is up by her left shoulder, and we only need six to eight inches of lift at the most to get her out. What if we double stack the airbag beside her arm and pull her out?"

"What about the other end, though? Don't you think it will shift when we start lifting?" Mack asked.

"No. I don't. I think it will just pivot in place if we only lift one side instead of the whole thing," Earl said.

"I agree," they both heard Dan say who was listening in from above.

They looked up to see Dan through the opening, giving them a thumbs up.

"Go with it. We're going to get started on a 3:1 haul line that we need to get you out. We can connect it to the sling and pull just enough to keep tension while you lift," Dan said.

"You have enough hands up there to man a 3:1?" Earl asked.

"More than enough. Word got out we found some live victims, so we have no less than an extra forty pairs of hands now," Dan said.

Dan and Evan got started on setting up the 3:1 system, which gave them a mechanical advantage when incorporated with a pulley, specifically a prusik minding pulley. A prusik was used as a friction hitch that could function as a brake for vertical lifts.

Earl positioned the stacked airbags next to Nadine under the concrete. At the same time, Mack connected the air cylinders and hoses to a manifold that acted as a controller to inflate or deflate the airbags.

Earl looked up to see Doug putting his pack back together. "Doug, you good?" he asked.

"Yeah. We're good. She has a liter of saline and an amp of D50 onboard now, and her pressure is coming up. Her neb should be done in a few. After that, I just need a five-minute warning so I can give her some Fentanyl before we move her," Doug explained.

"Will do," Earl confirmed.

"Earl, you ready for the strap?" Mack asked.

"Yeah. I'm ready." Earl answered.

Mack called Dan on the radio. "Dan, we are ready for that strap."

"Copy. I'm walking back up with it right now. Is the hole clear below?"

"Affirmative. The hole is clear. Drop it," Mack called back over the radio.

Mack picked up the strap and started back to where Earl was positioned next to the concrete. They worked together as they placed the girth hitch.

Mack looked up to see the end of the 3:1 lowering down and walked over to pull the slack out and hand it to Earl.

"Ok, Doug, this is your five-minute warning," Earl said.

Doug reached into his pocket and pulled out a syringe and connected it to Nadine's IV and slowly pushed the pain medication in. Afterward, he took another blood pressure to make sure that there were no side effects from the Fentanyl.

"Doug, we still good?" Earl checked.

"Still good," Doug said.

As he finished connecting the sling to the rope, Earl looked up to see Dan watching. "Dan, make sure you are only capturing the slack in the rope as we lift. With that 3:1, it will be easy to pull this down on top of her and us," Earl said.

"Got it. I'll be monitoring from right here," Dan said.

Before getting into position, to pull Nadine out, Doug

looked over at Stephanie. "Stephanie, you are next, ok? You still hanging in there?"

"I'm still hanging in there. Just take good care of Nadine."

"We sure will," Doug said.

Doug positioned himself behind Nadine's head, where he pulled the nebulizer mask off her face and turned off the oxygen. He then reached out and cupped his right hand under her right armpit. He would have to wait for the airbags to do their job before he could get a hold of the left one.

"Mack, you ready on the manifold?" Earl asked.

"Ready."

"Ok. We are going to go up on the bottom first, and if we need to, we will go up on the top one second." Earl explained.

"Copy that," Mack confirmed.

"Dan, we're starting," Earl yelled out.

"Roger that," Dan said as he watched from his perch above.

Earl gave the command. "Alright, Mack, lift the lower bag slowly."

Mack pushed the lever on the manifold, and air started to enter the lower bag as the concrete slab started to rise.

"Keep it going, Mack. Slow and steady. A little more. And...STOP!"

"Dan, hold on the haul line!" Earl yelled up to Dan.

"Holding," shouted Dan.

"Doug, how do we look from your side?" Earl asked

"Good. I think another two inches should do it," Doug said.

"Ok. Mack, instead of rounding out the bottom bag with more air, let's start going up on the top bag. It will be more stable that way," Earl explained.

"Top bag. Copy that. Say when," Mack said, moving his hand to the other lever.

"Dan, you ready on the haul line?" Earl asked.

"We are ready," Dan answered.

"Copy that, Dan. Remember, capture only what we are lifting with the rope and nothing more, or it will get pulled over on us, and Nadine," Earl confirmed.

"Got it, Earl. Just pulling the slack from the sling as you lift." Dan answered.

"Go," Earl called out.

Earl watched closely as the top bag began inflating, and the concrete started its rise again.

"Doug, talk to me," Earl said, not taking his eyes off the airbags.

"Almost there, Earl," Doug said. Doug watched closely as the concrete moved, and he noticed that the bottom of the slab was pulling on Nadine's shirt sleeve.

"STOP!" Doug shouted as he reached his left hand underneath the slab and tore the shirt free of the concrete.

"She's free," Doug confirmed as he placed both hands under Nadine's arms and pulled her body out from underneath the slab.

"All clear. We're all clear," Doug said.

He sat on the ground with his back resting against a desk flipped over on its side. Nadine laid across Doug's lap, slumped over in his arms. "That's a girl, Nadine. That a girl. Don't give up on us. Just a little further now."

Doug temporarily lost focus, but Earl and Mack didn't. They still had a two-ton problem they had to finish with.

"Doug, stay there with her until we get this lowered back down, and we will help you get her packaged for the ride out," Earl said.

"Got it," Doug said.

"Doug, you good?" Mack asked.

Doug patted the top of his helmet twice with his hand in response to Mack. The double pat on the head was a colloquialism in the tech rescue world to let others know you are good, or message received.

Doug gently moved Nadine to the ground, taking extra care with her left shoulder and arm. He then placed electrodes on her chest and connected her to a cardiac monitor to see if she was hyperkalemic. He didn't see any peaked T waves on the EKG, which meant for the time, no potassium was racing back to her heart.

After safely lowering the concrete back down, Earl and Mack helped Doug get Nadine packaged into the Stokes basket to be lifted out. They put a cervical collar on her to protect her neck and splinted her arm to her side to keep it immobilized. Doug reached down ad pulled a small piece of tape off by her IV.

"Let me disconnect the fluids from the lock before we start. I don't want it getting ripped out during the lift," Doug said.

After securing the IV, Doug stepped forward and connected his harness into the system so he could ascend with Nadine and the Stokes basket.

A Stokes basket was designed for use when there were obstacles to movement or other hazards such as confined spaces. Constructed in a tapered shape that is wider at the top and narrower at the legs, injured victims were typically placed in the Stokes on a backboard, with a cervical collar on their neck for immobilization and to prevent further injuries while being extricated. Rescuers would secure the victims to the basket using webbing or specialized straps. Ropes and carabiners could fasten to the basket to either lift it out in a horizontal or a vertical position, depending on how much room rescuers had to work with, and could allow for a rescuer to attach as an attendant.

"Do me a favor and send my bag up when the line comes back down. I need to check another Dexi and give her some IV antibiotics up top," Doug said.

"Will do," Earl said, patting Doug on the back. "You ready?"

"Ready," Doug confirmed.

Earl looked up and yelled at Dan to haul. Slowly Doug and Nadine ascended towards the sunlight shining down into the small cavern they felt like they had been in for days. For Nadine, it was the literal truth.

Dan watched from above as they got closer and closer to the top. "A little more. Haul. Haul. Haul. Stop!" Dan called out as he held up a closed fist.

Several eager bystanders helped as both Nadine and Doug came out of the hole.

"I think they want to help carry her down," Dan said with a hint of a smile.

"Yeah. Of course. I'll just follow behind to make sure they are careful," Doug said.

"Doug, take a blow down there and water up. We got more work to do," Dan said.

"Copy," Doug said tiredly as he took his helmet off and squinted at the sunlight, adjusting from being in the dark.

He followed behind as Nadine was passed down the middle of two lines of bystanders. They all cheered as she went from one set of hands to the next.

Doug looked at her arm from a distance as they descended, and he knew that if it didn't come off, she wouldn't survive.

They reached the bottom, and Doug had the volunteers set her down so he could do a full assessment and administer some IV antibiotics. As he was opening his pack, he noticed a shadow rush up from behind him.

"Nadine! Nadine! Oh my God, she's alive," Liezel exclaimed.

Doug moved to the side so Liezel could get closer.

"Oh, my sweet little girl, you are alive." Liezel knelt beside her and gently placed her forehead on Nadine's and wept.

Doug stood back and quietly watched.

He waited a few minutes and walked up beside the basket and knelt to give Nadine antibiotics while trying not to disturb Liezel. As he was pulling the medicine from his pack, he felt himself being yanked forward and squeezed by Nadine's mom.

"You are her angel. Nadine's guardian angel. I can never say thank you enough."

She released Doug from her strong embrace to look at him with tears in her eyes. Her attention was suddenly drawn to Doug's last name on his blue BDU shirt.

"Mr. Ditrichson?" She mispronounced it.

Doug gave her a soft smile. "Yeah, it's a tough one. You can call me Doug.

"Bless you, Doug," Liezel said.

"Thank you, but I wasn't alone," Doug said modestly.

"Thanks to all of you," Liezel said as she pulled Doug in for a second hug.

As he was being hugged again by Liezel, Doug noticed that Nadine was attempting to open her eyes. He pulled himself away to look down at Nadine.

"Nadine, can you hear me?" Doug asked.

Nadine shook her head as much as the cervical collar would allow her to. She tried to focus on him but only saw his silhouette against the hot afternoon sun behind them.

He pulled back as Liezel got close to talk to her and reached in his bag to get another liter of IV fluids and antibiotics to administer to her.

Doug felt a tap on his shoulder and turned to see Dr. Hollaway. "Hey, Doc. When did you get here?"

"About twenty minutes ago with Blue Squad. They have a real tough rescue they are working on over there by the collapsed stairs. I heard Red One did a great job."

Doug shrugged his shoulders. "Well..."

"Don't be modest, Doug," urged the doc. "Just take the compliment."

"Yeah. Thanks, Doc."

Doc paused to look around the university. "I have been on this team a long time, and we have never been on a deployment like this. It will be one for the books to be sure," he said.

A white pick-up truck backed up to where they were standing, and a group of bystanders picked Nadine up and placed her into the bed, followed closely by Liezel. Liezel blew Doug a kiss, and he blew one back.

"Do you know where they are taking her, Doc?" Doug asked.

"I don't," Doc said.

"If that arm doesn't come off, she is going to die," Doug said, watching them load Liezel into the back.

"I know. But Doug, remember this... we only control the process, not the outcome. Also, no more victims are being allowed into the embassy," Doc said.

Doug looked confused.

"Have you talked to Ron?" Doc asked.

"No. Not since he relieved me, what's up?" Doug asked.

"Claudette went into full crush syndrome when Ron pulled her out, peaked T waves and all. She is now on a dialysis machine at the embassy. The ambassador is concerned that the embassy could be overrun with patients and not having the resources to assist," Doc explained.

Doug's radio started to crackle. "Doug from Dan. We need you back up here. They are ready to do the airbag lift on Stephanie."

"Copy," Doug replied.

Doug turned to start walking back up the rubble pile and noticed off to the left that the pile of bodies had nearly doubled since he first arrived. He just shook his head.

He worked his way back to the top, weaving through the bystanders, where Dan was waiting.

"Did you water up down there?" Dan asked.

"No. I got distracted. Hey, how long was I down there in the hole?" Doug asked.

"I kind of lost track of time myself, but hours," Dan answered.

"Really? It seemed like we were working faster."

"For what you guys had to do, you worked fast enough," Dan replied.

Doug took the rope and connected it back into his harness.

"Water..." Dan said, smacking Doug on the helmet with a bottle.

"I want you to drink two right now and bring some more down for Earl and Mack," Dan prodded.

"Copy," Doug said.

"If you flake out down there, I'm going to let Mack start an IV on you," Dan threatened.

Doug choked on his water. "Mack can't spell IV."

Dan laughed and turned down the pile toward Evan. "On rope," Dan yelled down.

"On belay," Evan yelled back.

Doug touched back down in the hole where he went to work on Stephanie.

Earl walked back over to Doug with the oxygen bottle. "Hey, your PSI on this thing is pretty low," Earl said, showing him the gauge.

"I think we have enough to get another neb in her," Doug said.

Doug set his bag down and pulled out another neb mask and Albuterol. He unscrewed the chamber that connected to the bottom of the mask, pouring the Albuterol in and reconnecting the oxygen tubing before handing it to Earl.

"You mind getting that started on her. I need to look for an IV site," Doug asked.

"Got it," Earl answered.

Doug walked around and knelt with his bag in front of Stephanie. Reaching out, he gently put his hand on her left wrist to check her pulse. "Hey, Stephanie. You didn't think we would forget about you now, did you?" Doug asked with a smile.

Stephanie let out a small laugh. "No. I have faith in you guys. I listened to your work getting Nadine out and..."

She started to get choked up. "It was wonderful...You guys must really love people."

Doug, Earl, and Mack stopped what they were doing and looked at each other. Even if they wanted to say something, they couldn't. They were speechless. Blank ticker tape ran through their collective heads.

"Thank you, Stephanie." That was all Doug could think of to dignify her simple but powerful words.

"I'm going to start an IV now on your arm and give you some fluids and medicine that will help after we move this concrete off of you," Doug informed her.

"Ok," Stephanie said.

Doug continued. "And right before we lift, I am going to

give you some pain medicine that might make you feel a little woozy or sleepy. Understand?"

"I do. Thank you," Stephanie said.

"Mack, you want to give me that sterile water again so I can clean her arm up?" Doug asked.

"I'll clean it up. Go ahead and get your stuff ready," Mack said.

"Thanks, Mack," Doug said. Doug moved back into position and placed the tourniquet on her arm.

"You want another 20-gauge?" Mack asked.

"Actually, no. I'll take an 18-gauge this time. She has a decent vein here," Doug answered. Doug took the catheter from Mack and unsheathed it.

"Ok, Stephanie, you're going to feel a little pinch here," Doug informed her.

"Go ahead. I'm ready," Stephanie answered.

Doug glided the catheter into the vein and got a flashback but couldn't get it to advance completely. "I think I'm up against a valve. Earl, can you pick up the fluids and slowly open it and see if we can float this through?" Doug asked.

Earl opened the fluids, and Doug could see the blood from the flashback flow back into the arm as he gently pushed the catheter forward.

"I think it's in," Doug said, studying Stephanie's arm to

make sure there was no swelling that would indicate a blown vein.

He turned and looked up at the drip chamber on the IV tubing. It was flowing. "Good. Mack, do me a favor and get another pressure over palp on her other arm," Doug asked.

Doug finished securing the IV in place as Mack got the blood pressure.

"I'm getting around 110," Mack called out.

"I like that. I'm going to give her some crush meds along with this liter and let the Albuterol finish. After that, we can reassess and do the lift," Doug said.

"You want the D50 now?" Mack asked.

"Yeah. You know where it is?" Doug asked, looking back at his pack.

"Yep," Mack answered.

Mack took the D50 out of its box. D50 came in two parts. One was the actual long tubular vial that contained the D50 itself, and the other part was the syringe that the vial screwed into. Both parts had protective caps on them that got flipped off by using one's thumbs, famously illustrated at the opening of every episode of Emergency.

Mack held each part in separate hands and flipped the caps off with his thumbs. "Mack, AKA Mack Gage..."

Doug shook his head and smiled. Earl just looked at him like he was an idiot.

"Sorry, Stephanie. We have a little show going on over here, and we didn't bring you any popcorn," Doug said.

She didn't respond. "Stephanie?" Doug said, gently shaking her hand.

"Yes... I'm sorry. I'm really tired," she said groggily.

"I understand. We'll have you out of here soon."

Doug, Earl, and Mack took a short break to drink some water and allow time for Stephanie's IV fluids to flow into her body. Doug also wanted to allow for some time for the Albuterol and D50 to work on the potassium.

"Earl, get another pressure and pull the neb mask off," Doug asked.

Doug pulled out a smaller syringe and drew up the Fentanyl while Earl was taking the blood pressure.

"Close to 130. Maybe just a little lower," Earl told Doug.

"Aright. Good deal," Doug said.

"Ok. Stephanie, I'm going to give you some medicine now that might make you a little more tired, but it will help with the pain. Here we go," Doug said as he slowly administered the pain medication through Stephanie's IV.

Doug waited a couple of minutes to let the pain medicine work. "Stephanie. You still with us?" Doug asked, looking down at her.

"Yeah," she said in a groggy voice.

"Alright, guys, three minutes, and we can do the lift. After we get her out, let's get her on the monitor, and then we can package her," Doug said.

"Roger that," Earl answered.

"Same positions as last time," Earl instructed. "Mack, we're going to go up on both bags at the same time."

"Got it," Mack confirmed.

Doug put his pack out of the way and positioned himself by Stephanie's head.

"You two ready?" Earl asked.

"Ready," both Earl and Doug answered.

"One, two, three–up on both slowly."

"Earl, I can't see over there. You need to tell me when she is clear," Doug said.

"Yeah. Just a few more inches," Earl answered back.

Mack kept both hands on the manifold as the bags continued to inflate.

"Ten more seconds, Mack," Earl called out. Earl continued counting down. "Three, two, one...stop!"

Earl ducked down to shine his light under the concrete.

"I see some dry blood here. Not a lot, but it's causing her pant leg to stick to the rubble. I think she has an open tib/ fib fracture," Earl said, looking over to Doug.

"Earl, switch places with me really quick," Doug said as he got up to move.

Doug got down on all fours to get a better look at what Earl was telling him. He took out his trauma shears and carefully cut her pant leg free from the concrete. Afterward, he noticed that her pants had a strange twist to them. He repositioned so he could lay down flat on his stomach and shine his light back on her foot.

"Your right Earl. It's an open tib/fib. Her toe points in the opposite direction of her leg," Doug said.

Doug looked up to see if Dan was there at the opening. He wasn't. He keyed his radio, "Dan, from Doug."

"Go," Dan replied.

"I need you to drop a lower leg splint down to us."

"Copy. In the site box?" Dan asked.

"Affirmative," Doug answered.

Doug took a few more moments to think about what he wanted to do when they all of the heard pieces of rubble dropping and then a loud crash.

Doug and Mack instinctively curled up into balls and covered their heads. Earl covered Stephanie's body with his own and put his arms over his head. Then there was silence. There were no vibrations, no tremors, just silence.

The three of them slowly raised their heads and started to look around.

Dan raced to the opening where he could see small wisps of grey dust slowly billowing out.

"EARL, DOUG, JOHNNY! Are you ok?" Dan yelled down.

"Yeah, we're all good," Earl hollered back.

"What the hell was that?" Dan asked, trying to wave the dust away from him to get a better look down in the hole.

As the dust slowly cleared, Earl could see that the concrete slab they lifted off of Nadine was no longer there.

"I think that was the sound of Nadine's clean living," Earl answered.

"Come again?" Dan asked.

"The concrete that we lifted off of Nadine fell and pulled a few more pieces down with it," Earl answered.

Dan let out a long breath. He turned to look at Evan and gave himself a double tap on the helmet to let him know everything was ok.

"Alright. Let's get a move on. I want Stephanie and you guys out of that hole ASAP!" Dan said with urgency.

"Copy! Did you toss down the splint already?" Earl asked.

"I just dropped it," Dan answered.

"You two stay put; I'll go grab it," Doug said, standing up.

Doug returned with the splint and opened his pack and pulled out a roller gauze.

"Alright, here is the plan. Earl, you and I will pull her out just enough to clear the slab and stop. Mack, as soon as we move her, deflate the airbags, so that becomes a non-issue. Earl, before we move her leg off this slab, I need to realign it and splint it, and you guys know the rest after that."

Doug looked at both Earl and Mack and got a nod.

"Ok, Earl... on three. One, two, three," Doug counted off.

Doug braced Stephanie's lower leg as much as possible as Earl pulled her out. Stephanie moaned in pain as she was moved.

"I'm sorry," Earl said. "We're almost done.

Doug watched to make sure her foot was clear of the slab and told Mack to deflate.

"Ok, Mack, going to need your help over here," Doug said.

Mack moved into position next to Doug.

"I need you to stabilize her thigh as I realign her lower leg," Doug instructed.

"Got it," Mack confirmed.

This wasn't the first time Doug had to realign a lower leg. During his second season as a ski patroller, he responded with a sled for a wreck that took place on one of the intermediate trails. When he got on the scene, the skier was lying face up, but the toe of his boot was in the snow. Before he was able to realign it, he had to move the skier's ski pant legs around to see which way they were twisted to make sure he turned the leg back in the right direction.

"Stephanie, I'm going to move your leg now so we can splint it before we take you out of here," Doug said.

She didn't answer.

"Alright, Mack, here we go," Doug said.

Doug grabbed her lower leg and gently pulled traction on it to prevent the bone ends from hitting each other and then rolled it back over in line with the rest of her leg.

Stephanie let out a loud moan in pain and then fell silent again.

They quickly got her leg splinted and moved into the Stokes. Stephanie would moan in pain each time they moved her, but that was it. The Fentanyl was clearly doing its job.

The rope was waiting for them as the three of them moved her into position. Earl hooked both Stephanie and Doug into the rope system.

Earl patted Doug on the helmet. "Ready?"

"Ready," Doug confirmed.

"Dan, we're on rope!" Earl hollered up.

"Copy. On rope," Dan said, turning around, giving Evan the signal to haul.

Doug slowly left the ground with Stephanie as Dan watched from above.

Earl gave Mack a backhand to his chest. "C'mon pinhead. Let's get our gear together so we can get out of here.

Up above, the stokes basket reached the top where Dan, and even more bystanders than there were before, grabbed hold of it and Doug and pulled them free of the hole.

They all started cheering again the same way they did when Nadine came out as Dan was unhooking Doug from the rope.

"You need to follow her down?" Dan asked.

"Yeah. I need to do a quick secondary before we hand her off," Doug replied.

Again, he followed the Stokes basket down between the bystanders as they all cheered. After setting her down, he reconnected the IV that he took off for extrication and took another blood pressure.

"Stephanie? Can you hear me?" Doug asked, gently shaking her shoulder.

She moaned, turned her head toward Doug, and slowly opened her eyes.

"Hey there. How is the pain?" he asked.

Stephanie's eyes darted around in confusion. "Where am I?" she asked.

"You're out, Stephanie. We're outside the hole. You're safe," Doug answered.

She reached up and grabbed Doug's hand firmly and started to cry.

"I... I can never thank you enough," she said through her tears.

"I tell you what... the next time you see Nadine, you tell her the guys said, 'hi.'"

More tears started to fall as another pick-up truck backed in to transport Stephanie away.

Several bystanders approached them and started to pick her up.

"The leg. Be careful with her leg," Doug said firmly, making sure they knew what he was talking about.

Doug watched as she was driven off, then walked back up to the top. Earl was just clearing the hole with the help of Dan as he returned. Doug unhooked him and lowered the rope back down to Mack.

"She make it out, ok?" Earl asked.

"Yeah. They took her away in the back of a truck the same way they did with Nadine."

"Not in Virginia anymore, are we?" Earl said.

"Mmm, we are not," Doug replied as he was looking down to see if Mack was on rope.

"Mack, you ready?" Doug asked.

"Yeah. Haul!" Mack yelled up.

Dan turned around and gave Evan the signal to pull along with all the bystanders, happy to do anything to help.

Doug watched as Mack slowly ascended back to the top of the hole. As he neared, Mack had a big grin on his face.

"You have to admit; the Mack-Gage thing was pretty good, huh?"

Doug stared. "Shut up before I cut the rope."

GET IN LINE

Riley walked into the command tent to see Brian seated in front of a laptop looking at pictures.

"Are those from the field?" Riley asked.

"Yeah. Tech info guys set it up so the squads could use it as a photo cache. Have you had a chance to look at it yet?" Brian asked.

"Not yet," Riley answered.

Brian turned around to face Riley. "I'm amazed that we are pulling out anyone that is still alive. I've never seen this much destruction, and it seems like there is no end to it."

"You wish you were still on the squads?" Riley asked with a revealing grin.

"I didn't think I was that obvious," Brian said as he turned back around to scroll through more pictures.

"Speaking of squads, we finally got into a rotation. Red One and Blue One are in the BOO, and the other two are out working separate sites," Riley said.

"Good deal. They need some rest," Brian answered.

"Yeah. They are over in the rec center lined up for showers right now."

"Hey, did Mike say anything about those washing machines getting here anytime soon?" Riley asked. "Their uniforms literally smell like death."

"Nope," Brian said as he stood up and took a long stretch with his hands about his head.

"As of right now, we need to keep using the trash cans with laundry detergent and mop handles. But, do me a favor and listen for my sat phone for a spell. I need to go take care of a pressing matter."

"Pressing matter, huh?" Riley laughed.

"Yeah," Brian replied. Sounds way more sophisticated than code brown."

Brian turned and walked out of the command tent, making his way across the compound toward the rec center. As he entered, he saw a line coming out of the door from the men's locker room and laughter coming from inside.

"Nice to see you guys are not too tired for a good laugh," Brian said, walking in.

As he scanned the bathroom to see who all was in there, he couldn't help but notice a pickaxe, a clothes hanger, and a digging bar on the floor by the stall. *I know I should just turn around and walk away.*

But he didn't. "What's with the tools on the floor? You guys didn't get enough work out there that you have to have a drill?"

"Drill?" Mack snickered. "We have to drill something out of Doug's ass."

The bathroom erupted in laughter again.

"I think the Chinese call it hung chow. Ain't that right, Doug?" Mack continued between laughs. Brian just shook his head.

Dan started to chime in, trying to talk over the laughter.

"Hey Doug, help me out again. What were your exact words when you went in that stall over three hours ago? Something like you couldn't drive a straight pin up your tail with a ball ping hammer?"

Now Brian was laughing.

The laughter died down as they heard the latch open to the stall, and Doug walked out with his pants still around his ankles. Shuffling his feet, he walked right past Brian and out the locker room door.

"It's all yours, Chief," Doug murmured as he went by.

Brian watched as Doug made a left out the door shuffling down the hallway, walking into the ladies' locker room with not so much as a knock on the door. The room fell silent as all their eyes widened.

Dan was fighting to find the words. "Did he just...did he just go into...?"

Brian was still looking down the hall. "Yeah, he did...with his pants around his ankles."

Mack started hyperventilating and fell on the floor. Dan, Evan, and Earl, as well as few others from the blue squad, were not far from joining him.

In a failed attempt to keep a straight face, Brian pointed his finger at Dan. "I swear on everything good and holy if there was a female in that locker room when Doug walked in... you get to write it up."

After that, Brian stopped talking. He knew he was powerless at that point, but he knew if there was ever a group of men that needed a good laugh, it was them. Brian paused for a little while longer to take it in and then turned and left.

"Should we go check on Doug? Maybe we should bring the search cam over there so he can get a better look," Mack mused.

"Let it go, Mack. I think he is seriously hurting," Dan said as he was bending over to pick up the tools.

Dan was right. Doug was in a hurt locker. So much so, he failed to realize that when he entered the ladies' locker room, the lights automatically came on as he opened the door. And then they turned back off a few minutes later.

"Stupid lights," Doug said under his breath as he sat in misery.

He reached forward and unlocked the door to the stall to wave in back and forth, hoping it would be enough motion to get the lights to turn back on, but he wasn't so lucky. He groped his way off the commode where he took a few steps, pants still around ankles, waving his hands over his head in the dark—still nothing.

Just a few steps further, and that should....

The door swung open, and the lights came back on as Heather entered the bathroom.

"Oh! Oh! I'm sorry. I thought I was in the..."Heather blurted out before running out of the ladies' locker room.

Doug gave her time to make it down the hall before he exited the locker room himself and returned to the men's locker room–his pants still around his ankles.

***

"Mack, if you don't stop shaking my bunk, I'm going to jam a syringe into your temple," Doug exclaimed. The bed didn't stop shaking. Doug took a swing and didn't connect with anything.

Doug shot up off his bunk. "Mack, I'm going to..."

His bunk was still shaking, but no one else was in the tent with him. He was alone.

The tent swayed back and forth as Doug stumbled toward

the door and made his way outside as the shaking stopped. He saw Mack stopped in his tracks on his way back from the showers with a towel wrapped around his neck. Doug and Mack started walking toward each other when they saw Dan and Evan coming out of the command tent.

"Where's Earl?" Dan asked, walking over to meet them.

"He's getting out of the shower now," Mack answered.

"What was that?" Doug asked. "A big tremor or a small quake?"

"I think it was a big tremor," Dan said as he was looking down at his GPS.

"You got a Richter scale on that thing or something?" Doug asked as he watched Dan studying the GPS.

"That would be a nice feature, but no. I am looking at where they are sending us, and Doug, you'll like this," Dan said with a smile.

"Is that sarcasm?" Doug quipped.

"Not this time. A Navy chopper is picking us up in about 30 minutes and fly us north to do void searches at a convent," Dan said. Doug smiled. Dan knew that he was an aviation nut and loved to fly.

Before Doug went to work for the fire department, he worked as a flight medic in D.C., and he would get as giddy as a kid on Christmas morning whenever they got a mission. The hospital-based flight program was located only miles from the White House, and as such, required special flight patterns to keep them out of the prohibited air space. They called it splitting the "P's" when they flew between the White House and the Naval Observatory, where the Vice President lived. The flights Doug enjoyed the most were those going down into Virginia where they had to avoid commercial air traffic going into Reagan National. They would take off from the base, split the P's, and drop down over the Potomac River and turn south. Once over the river, they would play hopscotch with the bridges leading into and out of D.C. to maintain their clearance. It was difficult for Doug to keep himself from raising his hands in the air like he was on a roller coaster and yell, "Wee."

"I thought you might like that," Dan said, reading Doug's face. "And just so you know, Mack drew the short straw. So, if you need an in-flight enema, he's the one that will give it to you."

They were still laughing when Earl walked up. "What did I miss?"

"Nothing," Evan said. "Just some leftovers from yesterday. You guys get dressed and grab your packs. We'll meet over by the command tent in 15."

As the three of them returned in uniform and packs on, Doug stopped to pick up some water and MREs. "Tell Dan I'll be there in a second."

Dan stood outside the command tent with Brian, Riley,

a dog handler with her dog, and a couple of military personnel.

"Here comes the rest of Red Squad One. Where's Doug?" Brian asked, looking behind them.

"He's right behind us, Chief," Earl answered.

"Ok," Brian started. "This is Heather. She is a new handler on the team, and beside her is Thor.

Thor sat perfectly next to Heather's feet with his unattended leash lying on the ground.

"The two of them will be flying out with you today, along with Steve and Carlton. Steve and Carlton are Air Force Pararescue and will be your force protection. Heather, Steve, Carlton, you met Dan and Evan. This is the rest of Red Squad One: Earl, Mack, and..."

"Sorry, Chief. Got held up," Doug said as he joined the briefing.

"No worries—just making introductions. And this is their med spec. Doug," Brian said as he finished.

Doug exchanged handshakes with Steve and Carlton, then turned to shake hands with Heather, which caused him a momentary pause. A shy grin started to form across Heather's face, which did not go unnoticed by Brian.

"Did you two already meet?" Brian asked.

"Yeah, Brian. I bumped into Doug yesterday in the uh–rec center," Heather replied.

"So, this is the deal," Brian continued. "We are sending you up to search a convent. They are missing three nuns. Right now, they are presumed to be dead, but they want to be sure. I already explained that we could not guarantee they can be located based on the heavy damage they have. Heather will run Thor first before we search, so we don't mess up the scent. If he does not give her any alert, we will start with void searches and Delsar. If you find a live victim that requires technical breeching, the helicopter will come back for the tools. Copy?" Brian asked.

"Copy," everyone said together.

"Also, be prepared to be pulled off and flown out if we get confirmation of a live rescue at a different location.

"And finally, be smart about the risks you take. We all felt that aftershock we just had. Remember, we are still in rescue mode, not recovery. We clear?"

They all responded collectively as the thumping sounds of helicopter blades could be heard approaching in the distance.

MARTHA, MARIE, AND MARY

The helicopter touched down in a clearing just 300 feet outside the rear gates to the embassy. One by one, they loaded up, taking any empty jump seat. Doug was the second to last on, just in front of the crew chief. He turned to find an empty seat, which was easy since there was only one left–right beside Heather.

Perfect. Doug flashed a quick smile with a nod as he sat down next to Heather. Thor stood up and began sniffing at Doug, starting at his boots and working is way up to his knees where he stopped and just stared at him.

"Are you a dog lover?" Heather asked loudly, trying to speak over the sound of the helicopter.

"Actually, I am," Doug said as he continued to stare down at Thor.

"I figured, she said genially. "Thor has a sixth sense when it comes to that."

"Is it ok to pet him?" Doug asked.

"Sure. That's what he is waiting for. Do you have a dog?" Heather asked.

Doug reached down and let Thor sniff him before scratching him on of the head. "Yeah. I have an American Brittany."

"Do you hunt?" Heather asked.

"Nope. Just like the breed. They have a lot of energy and love people and other dogs. Sometimes he is more than I can handle around the house, but out in the woods, off-leash, something clicks. He becomes a different dog. He is more attentive and obedient off-leash. Crazy, huh?"

"Does your dog have a name, or do you just call him 'He'?" Heather asked with a smile.

Doug laughed, "Reagan. His name is Reagan."

"Well, Reagan is a working dog just like Thor, and when he is in the field, he feels like he is doing his job. Which makes sense since that is what he was bred for. It's no different than when Thor is on the rubble pile or doing searches."

Doug continued petting Thor. "I guess I never really thought about it like that. Is he ready for today?"

"Thor? Yes. Me? No," Heather answered, sounding apprehensive.

The rotor blades started to spool up from their idle speed,

and the helicopter slowly lifted off and turned toward the north.

Doug could tell Heather was uneasy, but she had a right to be since it was her first deployment and her first time going out with a squad. "Well, let me tell you this, Heather. I can tell you are a little nervous, and I would be concerned if you were not, especially being on your first mission. It tells me you are more focused on doing a good job, and not as concerned about putting on a good show just to impress us. And as long as I am being honest, I have more concern about the pilot than you."

"Pilot?" Heather said, looking up at the cockpit.

"Yeah. He looked really glassy-eyed, like he had one too many at the officer's club last night. I bet chances are he will fly us into a hillside before we get to the convent anyway," Doug deadpanned.

"Yeah, right. I thought the same thing," Heather said with a straight face. "He looks like he had so much to drink; he probably walked into the ladies room by mistake."

Doug dropped his head and laughed. "Touché...but about that..."

Heather held up her hand. "I really am not looking for an explanation. Seriously though, I appreciate it. I know what you are trying to do, and it worked. I'm ready to get started."

"That's what I'm talking about..." Doug said with a big smile.

The crew chief sat next to Dan and tapped him on the leg to get his attention so he could put on his Dave Clark headphones that allowed him to talk to the pilot.

"Yes, sir," Dan said after putting the headphones on.

"Our landing site looks good, but it could be more level. So, after we land, keep your team seated, and we'll shut down for a cold offload. We should be on the ground in a few minutes.

"Rodger that. Thank you, sir." Dan took off the headphones and gave them back to the crew chief.

The pilot banked left and started his descent. Dan propped himself up against the fuselage so he could get a lookout at the convent. Red Squad One watched Dan as he assessed what lay below. Dan could be a hard read sometimes, but they knew it wasn't good.

Dan, Evan, and Carlton jumped off after shutting down and walked up to the convent, where three nuns awaited them next to an exterior stairway that led up into the main entrance where a single portion of the exterior wall that remained standing with not much keeping it that way. It didn't go unnoticed by Dan and Evan.

"Hey Dan, let's move this meet and greet away from that wall," Evan said in a hushed voice as they got closer.

"Uh, huh," Dan replied, coming to a stop about 50 feet away from where the nuns stood. Dan looked over the area of the building that collapsed, and it reminded him of Montana, only with fewer void spaces to search.

"This is more pancaked than the Montana," Evan said, stopping alongside Dan.

"Yeah. Let's give it our best. If we can at least get an idea of where the missing nuns are, it will be something they can caution the heavy machinery operators about when they come in to clear this out.

Dan motioned the nuns over to where he was standing. They walked up to Dan and Evan and took both of their hands and kissed them.

"Bless you for coming. The people of Haiti are so grateful for all you have done," said one of the nuns.

"Thank you, sister. My name is Dan, and this is Evan. "

"I am Sister Marie, and these are Sisters Martha and Mary."

Marie, Martha, and Mary. I'm sure I'll keep that straight. Dan paused, directing their attention back to the convent.

"I need to be honest with you. The way this has collapsed is not good. The floors are laying directly on top of one another, which does not create many void spaces where one would be able to survive," Dan explained.

The nuns shook their heads in understanding.

"I'm sure it's not what you wanted to hear, but I don't want to give you false hope," Dan continued.

"We know, and we are at peace with whatever the outcome is," said Sister Marie.

"Sister Marie," Evan quickly interjected, "Do you mind walking the rest of the team and us around to give us an idea of where you think they might have been at the time of the quake?"

"Yes. Certainly," Marie answered.

Evan turned and motioned for the rest of them to come up to the building.

"That's is our cue, Heather. All set?" Doug asked as he was putting his medical pack on.

"Yep. Let's get to work," she replied confidently.

They joined up with Dan and Evan as they started to walk around the convent counterclockwise. The sisters pointed out to the team where there was a small chapel located on side Delta.

"It's possible they could have been in there when it happened," Sister Mary pointed out.

"Are there any entrances directly into the chapel from the outside or hallways that lead into it?" Evan asked.

"Yes," Sister Marie answered. "Over on the front side of the building where we just were is a door that leads down a hallway to the chapel."

Dan nodded. "Ok. Heather, when you run Thor, let's check

quadrant Delta really well. Maybe they were trying to make their way down that hallway during the quake."

"Copy Dan," Heather said as she was making a simple sketch of the convent on a notebook.

Doug noticed a little pep in her step after Dan called on her. He knew that giving someone trust is the best way to build their confidence.

They turned the corner on the back of the convent, where the grade sloped away from the building. Halfway downside Charlie, another exterior wall remained standing with a very ominous lean toward the slope.

"Hey, Dan..." Evan called out.

"Yep. Got it," Dan came back. "Sister Marie, we are going to walk a few more yards and stop before we get to that wall, ok?"

"Oh, ok, Dan," she answered, coming to a stop.

"Can you tell us what is on the other side of that wall?" Evan asked.

"That is where the kitchen and dining room is located," Sister Martha answered.

"Is it possible for them to have been in there at that time of the day?" Dan asked.

"Possibly, but not likely," Sister Marie answered. "The sisters who would have been in there are accounted for."

"Ok. That's good," Dan said. Let's start walking back around to the front of the building the way we came and finish our primary recon over there."

They walked back around to the front, being careful to stay out of the collapse zone of the lone exterior wall that was still standing. From there, they continued around to the Bravo side, where half of the exterior wall remained intact.

"What was in this part of the building?" Dan asked.

Sister Marie turned to see what area Dan was asking about.

"Those are administrative offices. We already walked through there and did not find anything.

Dan raised his eyebrows. "Oh, ok. Well, I think it would be a good idea if we keep this area off-limits for your safety. If that front wall collapses, the floors that are attached to it are coming down too."

"We understand. We will not go back in there," Sister Marie said as they all shook their heads in acknowledgment.

"Hey Dan, I got a question if you don't mind?" Earl asked.

"Sure," Dan acknowledged.

Earl looked back over to where the chapel was located. "Is the ceiling of the chapel vaulted?"

Sister Marie shook her head. "Vaulted?"

Earl paused, thinking about the right words to describe what he was asking.

"Is the ceiling the same height as the rest of the first floor, or was it higher? Umm, was there a loft in the chapel?" Earl asked.

"Oh, yes. There is a loft in the back of the chapel. It's located on the second floor. And the ceiling, it's comes to a point, or a peak, I guess is the right word for it?"

Dan nodded his head. "Good question Earl. I should have thought of that."

Dan continued. "The reason he asked that is that depending on how the ceiling came down, it could have come to rest on other parts of the building such as walls and floors creating a survivable void. Again, it's only a possibility. And I cannot promise we will even be able to make our way in far enough to make that assessment.

"Of course. The last thing we want is for you to get hurt," Marie answered.

"Alright," Dan said, transitioning. "We are going to get started. Please stay away from these outside walls. If we have another aftershock like we had this morning, they could easily come down. And quite honestly, I am surprised they haven't already."

Sister Marie turned to point down a path that led away from the convent. "Down there is our living quarters. We will…"

"Is it damaged?" Dan interrupted.

"Oh, no. It's fine. It's a large wood building. I just want you to know where we will be if you need anything."

"Right. Thank you," Dan answered.

Dan turned to Heather. "I would like Thor to start on top of the pile, but it looks like he would need to go into the convent, and work is way up. You ok with that?"

"Sure," Heather said.

"When I ask if you are ok with that, I mean you stay out and send him in by himself," Dan said.

"Yeah. I figured as much, and my answer hasn't changed," assured Heather.

"Alright, then. Turn him loose," Dan said.

She kept Thor on his leash as she led him back around to the exterior stairs leading back into the convent. It was evident that Thor knew he was about to go to work. Heather came to a stop a safe distance away from the wall, and Thor immediately sat next to her without command. She reached down and unhooked his leash, and he didn't move an inch.

"Thor," Heather said, looking down at him. "Search!" she commanded, pointing at the stairs.

Thor dashed up the stairs and stopped to look back at Heather. She pointed up to the top of the pile. "Go!"

Thor disappeared over the top. Heather walked parallel with the front side of the building. Thor returned and looked back down at her. "Go!" And away he went again.

She continued this down the length of the building. Each time he would come back and look down at her, having covered more space.

Heather reached the end of the convent on the front side, and Thor came back and looked down at her.

"Thor, your nose better be working buddy," Heather said.

"Ok. If you're sure, then, back!" Heather commanded. She was nervous that he didn't alert on anything.

The rest of the squad sat in the shade, avoiding the hot, late morning sun. They sat in silence as they watched Thor work. They were impressed. It was clear that Heather spent a lot of time with this dog, and they were on the same sheet of music.

Less than a minute later, Thor ran back down the exterior stairs and turned left towards Heather, who was waiting for him at the corner of the building. As he was running, he began to alter his path away from Heather and in toward the building.

Heather got a frustrated look on her face. "Thor!" she shouted.

He ignored her. He ran right up to the building and ran his nose along the ground and stopped. Heather watched.

Thor then lifted his head so he could put his nose as high as he could in the air. He turned and did the same thing back the other direction and returned again. This time he raised up on his hind legs and placed his front paws on the convent and started barking.

NEW LOW FOR LOOTING

Heather ran to where Thor was alerting, and Red One hopped to their feet and started moving in the same direction.

A few feet above where Thor was barking was a small opening that extended back into the convent approximately forty to fifty feet. Earl shined a flashlight back into the darkness, but he couldn't see anything.

"What do you think, Earl?" Dan asked, looking on.

"It's doable," Earl answered. I think this might have been part of that entrance to the chapel."

"Ok. Earl, take Doug with you and see if you can get a closer look."

"Yeah, send Doug in. He's a veteran of living through aftershocks in tight places," Doug said with sarcasm. The squad laughed at him.

Earl reached up to where he was able to move a sizable piece of rubble that made access a little easier.

"Mack, be useful and turn yourself into a step stool," Earl said.

Mack dropped to all fours, and Earl stepped on his back and started to worm his way into the building.

As soon as Earl made his way in, Doug stood up on Mack's back and waited.

"Do you really need to wait on my back?" Mack asked, grunting.

"Safety first brother. I have to keep an eye on Earl. He sure is moving slowly, though," Doug joked.

About a minute later, Doug was able to start working his way into the building.

"Evan, hang here. I'm going to go over and talk to Carlton and Steve really quickly," Dan said as he turned to walk away. "Heather, you and Thor want to follow me?"

"Sure. C'mon Thor." Dan walked a few feet in silence until Heather and Thor caught up.

"You guys did well," complimented Dan.

"Thanks, Dan," Heather replied.

"I'm not used to seeing a dog return and look back the way he did. That's different," Dan said.

"It is," Heather replied. "But it's not on my account. It's like he wants to be told where to go – almost like a game to him. I have heard of other dogs that will do it, though."

"Pretty cool trait," Dan said as they reached PJs.

"You guys hang out here while we get to work over there. It's going to be 110 degrees today with the heat index. No need in all of us suffering. Enjoy the shade and stay hydrated."

"Will do," Carlton answered. "Let me know if you guys want a hand over there, though." Dan could tell he was itching to do anything.

"Ok. I'll keep you in mind," Dan answered.

Inside the convent, Earl and Doug worked their way back further. Earl stopped and started coughing.

"You good? Doug asked.

"You can't smell that?" Earl growled back.

"Smell wh…?" was all Doug could get out before he started doing the same thing.

"I think we are close to one of them," Earl said, trying not to breathe in.

"Something tells me it's more than one of them," Doug said, holding his nose.

Earl paused to move the light around on his helmet. A few feet in front of him, he could see an opening where he might be able to stand.

"Stay put. I'll move forward." Earl instructed. "We might have some more room up ahead."

"Copy," Doug said.

Earl continued ahead, slowly making his way through debris and shards of concrete. Reaching out in front of him, he was able to feel a drop off where he used both hands to pull himself forward. His helmet light concentrated straight down and reflected off the concrete until he reached the clearing where his light revealed a body.

"What the..." Earl said, getting spooked by the sudden appearance of the deceased victim.

"What is it?" Doug asked from behind.

"I uh, I found one. It's bad," Earl answered.

"How bad?" Doug asked.

"Her skin is sloughing off her skull," Earl replied.

"Ok. Wow," said Doug. "Umm, do you think we can get her out?"

Earl grunted as he pulled himself forward and gently tried to maneuver around the body. "Give me a second. I'm checking now."

The nun's body was positioned perpendicular to the hole that Earl had crawled through. Her legs extended out underneath another slab that sloped down from the floor above. Earl squatted down to focus his light on her legs to make sure they were free when he was distracted by a strange sound from about him.

"Pitttttth" was the sound he heard before Earl felt something hit his arm.

Looking up, Earl saw a leg sticking out three feet above him. It was bloated and oozing. He fought hard to keep his gears from reversing.

"Hey Doug," Earl called back with a strained voice. "Is it normal for swollen bodies to spit at you? Earl asked in a disgusted tone.

"Uh yeah. I've heard of it. Basically, they get swollen from the off-gassing, and the skin starts breaking." Doug answered. "Why? Did you get spit on?"

"I did, and I found the second nun. Pretty sure we are not going to be able to get her out, though," Earl answered.

"What do you need up there, Earl?" Doug asked.

"Holler out at Dan and let him know we found two, but only one is coming out."

"Ok. Anything else?"

"You bring any body bags?" Earl asked.

"I have one rolled up in my med pack, but that's the only one I have," Doug answered.

"Well, it's the only one we need right now," answered Earl.

"Copy," said Doug. Doug hollered out to Dan with an abbreviated situation report and told him to send someone in with the body bag.

"I'm going to move forward and help Earl place her in a bag. I need someone else to crawl in and pull her out when we are ready," Doug yelled out at Dan.

"Alright. Give me a few," Dan yelled back down the hole.

Dan turned and made his way back over to where Carlton, Steve, and Heather were standing by.

"Make sure Thor gets some extra Scooby snacks tonight. He found two of the nuns," Dan said, patting Thor on the head. "It's going to be a recovery, though."

"Oh," Heather said somberly.

"Hey, listen. Thor's find was important. You are giving them closure and allowing them to have a proper burial for at least one of the nuns," Dan said in a comforting tone.

Heather gave Dan a little nod in reply.

"Carlton, you still want to get your hands dirty," Dan asked.

"Sure do. Thanks," Carlton replied.

"Well, don't thank me too soon. I haven't told you what you are doing yet. Follow me back over," Dan said, turning to leave.

"Steve, you good?" Carlton asked.

"Yeah, I'm good. I'll hang out with Thor and Heather," replied Steve.

As they got closer, Dan explained to Carlton that he needed to take a body bag to Doug so he and Earl could place one of the nuns in there and pass it off to him to pull back out.

"You think you can handle this?" Dan asked.

"We'll find out," Carlton answered.

"You claustrophobic?" Dan answered.

"Not that I know of," Carlton replied.

"Well, if you get uncomfortable in there, just give us a heads up. No shame in it if it's not your thing. Our med spec hates it," Dan said.

Mack unzipped Doug's med-pack and pulled out the rolled-up body bag. "Dan, catch." Dan caught it and turned and handed it to Carlton.

"Hey, Carlton, one second before you go in. I know you are way outside my circle of influence and that you were assigned to us as force protection, but uh–I would really appreciate it if you took that M4 off your shoulder before you crawl in there," said Dan.

"That makes sense. We only got one body bag, anyway, right?" Carlton joked.

Dan laughed. "Yeah. Something like that."

Carlton started in and met up with Doug and passed the body bag. From there, Doug moved forward into the same opening where Earl waited.

"Oh, geez, that's bad," Doug said as he moved in beside Earl.

"I've never seen anything like it before, not in person anyway," Earl shared. "What do you think?"

"I think we have to be very careful or she will break open. I'm pretty sure you knew that much already. But what if we place the body bag over the top of her and scoop from underneath, so we don't have to move her directly? Does that make sense?"

"Yeah. Perfect sense," Earl agreed.

"Alright, I take the head and torso if you take it from the hips down," Doug said as he started to unfold the body bag.

They took the bag, unzipped it, and placed the opening over the top of the nun.

"I'm over her head. You have enough to cover the feet?" Doug asked, turning his light down toward Earl.

"I'm good," Earl answered.

"Ok. Count of three we scoop. One, two, three, and scoop," Doug said.

As they started scooping, an arm came out and hit Doug in the stomach, causing him to jump.

"What are you doing, Earl? I said to scoop so we don't tear the bag," Doug barked at Earl.

"I am scooping. You sure you didn't tear the bag?" Earl said indignantly.

"No look, my end is...what's going on?" Doug said, his voice trailing off.

Both Earl and Doug looked down at the bag, and it wasn't torn. They looked at each other then rolled the bag back over to see if there were two arms inside. There were.

"You have got to be freaking kidding me?" Doug said, shaking his head.

"What? What happened?" Earl asked.

"She is on top of the third nun Earl," Doug said.

"She's what?" Earl asked.

"Unless this nun has more arms than normal, she is laying on top of the third one," Doug explained.

They continued to work together, getting the nun into the body bag and zipped up. They repositioned the bag so they could pass it off to Carlton, who was waiting to remove her out of the building.

"Doug, you want to follow him out. I'm sure he will need help navigating the bag around all this debris," Earl asked.

"Sure. I got it," said Doug.

"Once we get her lifted out, I want to get a better look to see how trapped this third nun is," Earl said.

"Roger that," Doug answered.

"Carlton, you ready?" Doug asked.

"Yup," Carlton replied, only it sounded more like a burp.

"Dude, you ok?" Doug asked.

"Yeah... just a little worse than I expected," answered Carlton.

"Ok, brother. Hang tough, and we'll have you out in some fresh air real soon," Doug said, trying to encourage him.

"I'm good. Let's get back to work," said Carlton.

Doug and Earl lifted the nun out and passed her off to Carlton, who started working backward out of the building. A few minutes later, Carlton's feet appeared coming out of the hole. Mack helped lower him down.

"Take a blow; I got it from here," Mack said.

He reached up and grabbed the bag, and guided it out as Doug followed from the other end.

"Dan, can you grab the other end coming out?" Mack called out.

"I got it," Dan answered. Doug's hands reached out and passed the bag off to Dan.

Dan motioned with his head to Mack. "Let's carry her over and place her under that tree."

As they returned back to the building after carefully placing the nun, Earl was coming out.

"So, we found the third one?" Dan asked.

"Yeah, but way too entrapped to come out. It's not worth the risk," Earl said tiredly.

"Well, good job. It will mean a lot to the sisters," Dan said.

"Thanks, Dan," said Earl.

"Alright then, let's..." Dan started to say, and he stopped talking after a loud crack rang out through the air. Then it happened five more times only faster.

Carlton grabbed his M4 and took off running in the direction of the noise.

Everyone dropped to the ground except for Mack. "Hey guys, that sounded like gunfire," Mack said, still standing with a look of curiosity on his face.

"You think?" Earl yelled before grabbing Mack by the collar and slamming him to the ground.

"Heather!" Dan said as he started to move.

Evan grabbed him. "Steve is up there. She's fine."

Red Squad One stayed on the ground until Carlton returned a couple of minutes after the shooting had started.

"We're clear. Everyone is safe," Carlton said. They all got up and followed Carlton.

When they reached Steve and Heather, they saw three Haitian males lying on the ground, each resting in the opposite direction of the one next to them. The one in the middle had his hands zip-tied to the ankles of the outside two. The outer two had their hands zip-tied to the ankles of the one in the middle.

"Looters," Steve said. We heard some commotion coming from down the path, and they came running toward us. One of them was armed, so I fired a shot to get him to drop it, but he didn't. So, I fired several more in the air, and he dropped the pistol."

Dan looked at Heather. "You alright."

"I'm fine," Heather reassured. "Thor is a little worked up, though."

Dan looked down to see Thor flashing his pearly whites at the looters, and two of the three looters were looking back at Thor. He intimated them more than the PJ's M4s.

Dan looked at Steve with a pensive stare. "How did you know they were looters?"

Steve shrugged his shoulders. "Mostly a hunch. I just figured they weren't here for the gift shop."

Sisters Marie, Martha, and Mary walked up the path toward them with a security guard.

"Is everyone ok?" Sister Marie asked, out of breath.

"Everyone is fine," Carlton reassured her. Is your security going to handle this from here? I would like to move everyone away from this."

"Yes. Of course," Marie said.

Carlton led everyone away from the scene and back towards the helicopter. "Dan, Steve and I will wait over here for you," Carlton said.

"Copy," Dan answered. "Thanks."

Dan turned to face the sisters. "We were able to remove one of the nuns. We placed her under the tree over there. It looks like they were trying to get out of the chapel at the time of the quake. The other two were close by her."

The sisters started to weep.

"Sister Marie, there is more you need to know. The other two are severely trapped, and it would require a great deal of risk do remove them."

Sister Marie shook her head. "I understand. You shouldn't be endangering your lives when they are already gone to a better place."

"Is there anything else we can do for you before we leave?" Dan asked.

"No. You have done so much already. And I'm so sorry you had to be involved with the looting."

"Well, I have to admit, it will be memorable," Dan said with a smile.

The sisters laughed. "Look, you put smiles on our faces," Sister Mary said. "If you did nothing else here today, that would be enough."

They got hugs and blessings from all the sisters before making their way back to the helicopter.

They all piled back onto the helicopter and dropped down into the same jump seats they were in on the flight out. Thor laid on the floor next to Doug and was very intent on sniffing his legs and boots.

"He knows I'm alive right?" he asked Heather, looking down at Thor.

"Yeah. He knows the difference, but how do you get used to that smell?" She asked.

"You don't. It's virtually impossible to get out of your clothes too."

Heather leaned in toward Doug and whispered. "I'm calling dibs on the shower."

Doug shook his head and smiled. "You really are becoming quite the veteran."

PBJ

Dan quickened his pace after getting off the helicopter to catch up to Steve and Carlton.

"Hey guys, I didn't get a chance to thank you back there for what you did. We all were very impressed. Takes a special person to run toward the danger the way you guys did. Thanks for having our backs."

"You're kidding, right?" Carlton asked.

Dan was somewhat confused. "No. I just really appreciate having you there."

"No, we get that," Carleton responded. "It's your humility that is really baffling us right now."

"Humility...?" Dan questioned.

"Yeah. You know, a low estimate of one's self, self-abatement sort of thing?"

Carlton continued. "We have folks, more than not, that go a whole career in the military and never see any action. You guys see it just about every day you go to work.

You run into houses that are on fire, you tunnel under buildings that could collapse on you, you dismember deceased victims so you can save the live ones, and who knows what else?"

"I guess we really don't think of it like that," Dan replied.

Carlton laughed. "We know you don't. None of you do. That's what makes it so cool. And you know what Dan, I don't think we have anyone in the military that can do what you guys do, which is probably why they always send you."

"Well, just the same, we appreciate you being here," Dan said.

"Dan, at the end of the day, we both wear the same flag on our shoulders. Never forget that." Carlton remarked.

"I won't. Thanks again guys," Dan jovially responded.

"It was our pleasure," said Carlton. We'll catch up with you later. We have to go track down our C.O."

The sun was starting to set as Dan, the rest of Red One, and Heather made their way over to the command tent where Brian, Riley, and Mike were milling around outside.

"Hey, Red One," Mike called out as they approached. "I heard Heather was baptized by fire today, literally."

"You heard about that?" Dan asked. "I tried to call in on the sat phone but failed to get a signal that was strong enough."

"Steve and Carlton debriefed with the pilot while you were still talking to the nuns and then called it in," Brian answered. "Evidently, the military's radios are way better than ours."

"Dan, you got second?" Brian asked, motioning to the command tent.

"Uh, sure, Brian," Dan answered. "Guys, I'll catch up to you in a little bit. Heather, good job out there today."

"Thanks, Dan. Same to you guys."

Dan turned and followed the others into the command tent.

"Take a load off," Mike said, motioning to a chair.

"How's your squad holding up?" Riley asked.

"Fine. I mean, I know they are tired, but who isn't? But they are staying focused and working hard. No one is making any stupid decisions," Dan said.

"How's Doug?" Brian asked. "I don't mean to single him out, but he has had a lot thrown at him on this one."

"No. I get it," Dan answered. "He's hanging tough. If there is something stuck in his craw, he is doing a good job of covering it up or faking being ok. I think if something was up, we would have noticed it by now. And when I say we, I mean Red One."

"Good. That's all we needed to hear. I know you're not going to B.S. us." Riley answered.

"Is that it?" Dan asked

"Almost," Brian replied as he turned around to pick up a piece of paper of the desk behind him. "The ops center back home got a phone call from the Pentagon, and they informed us that there were quite a few of our own military personnel in the Montana when it went down."

Dan shook his head. Partly because he didn't like the news he was hearing, and partly because he knew where the rest of the conversation was going.

"We need to send Red One back up to the Montana tomorrow to be on standby for recovery. I know I told you this morning we were still in rescue mode, and I'm not sure why I told you that because I don't recall us ever going out the door without being in that mode. But it's different this time, Dan," Brian explained.

"Different is one word for it," Dan answered back.

"Yeah, listen, there will be a track hoe up there delayering. If they find a body, attempt to I.D. it with anything that might be in their pockets, bag them, and move them to the temporary morgue they have set up there. And Dan, it's going to be a nasty business. These victims have been trapped now for days on end in high temps, so keep an eye on your guys."

"Will do," Dan said.

"Dan," Riley added in, "We will send you out with a full complement of tools just in case you have a live find. And again, be prepared to get moved to another site if needed."

"Alright," Brian said, standing up. "Get out of here and get some rest. Again, tell the boys they did a good job today."

Dan got up and walked out of the tent without saying a word, but he didn't even realize he did. Just simply sitting in a chair for a few minutes was all it took to start shutting down after going so hard for so many days.

**

Earl and Doug were sleeping hard as their peaceful slumber was disturbed by the door of their tent slamming shut.

"GIVE IT BACK!" Mack raged.

They both roused a little, and just as fast they were awakened, they were back to sleep. Mack stormed down the length of the tent and kicked Doug's bunk, and after taking a few steps more, kicked Earl's.

"Where did you put it?" Mack demanded.

Earl sat up, rubbing his face and eyes with both hands while Doug rolled over to face the opposite direction of the annoying chatter.

"Mack, you better have a good reason for disturbing the best sleep I have had in a while," Earl said in a deep, growly, sleepy voice.

"Nice try slick, but this ain't my first rodeo." Mack cautioned. "Somebody is messing with me, and my money is on you two."

Doug rustled under his sleeping bag and cleared his throat. "Mack, you shouldn't use a singular noun when you are talking about two people."

"Mack, what is missing?" Earl asked, slinging his feet off his cot and onto the floor.

"My peanut butter and jelly! I'm not eating those MREs. I'll be locked up worse than Doug was!" Mack exclaimed.

"You sure it's not another squad trying to mess with you?" Doug said, rolling over to face him.

Mack studied them hard. *Nothing. Either they have the best poker faces in the world, or they're telling the truth.*

"I think they sent Blue Two and Red Two out last night. I would go check their tents to see if they have it," Doug said, standing up and taking a long stretch.

Mack turned and stormed out of the tent.

"Hey, you wearing a new uniform today or yesterday's?" Earl asked.

"Well, before I took a shower last night, I took off my uniform and laid it on the concrete to air out with the intention of wearing it today. I figured it wouldn't take long before the clean one smelled the same anyway," Doug answered.

"Yeah, I'm kind of thinking the same thing," Earl agreed.

They got dressed and headed out across the compound to join Dan and Evan, who were sitting on gearboxes rummaging through boxes of MREs looking for that perfect breakfast.

"Why is it they make an MRE for every meal known to man, but they can't make one for breakfast?" Dan said as he continued to sift through the boxes.

"Geez, you know we have showers," Dan said with a disgusted look as Earl and Doug sat down on gearboxes next to them.

"We took showers, but what's the point of putting on a clean uniform when we're going to do more recoveries?" Doug answered.

"Oh, I don't know, call it professional courtesy," Dan snapped back.

Mack walked up to the squad with a defeated look on his face.

"Any luck, Mack?" Evan asked.

"No. Big goose egg," Mack said.

"Well, it will turn up when whoever did it feels like you suffered enough," Evan said.

"I can't decide," Dan said with a blank stare. "Doug?"

"I don't care. Just toss me one," Doug answered.

"Earl?" Dan called out.

"Same. I just need to eat something," replied Earl.

"Evan?" Dan asked.

"Unless you have a western omelet with hash browns, just toss me one," said Evan.

Dan reached down into the same box and tossed Evan, Earl, and Doug an MRE.

"Hey Mack, here is a chicken and dumplings! I hear they are good," Dan said, trying to cheer him up.

Mack reached over and took it from Dan.

"Hey, Mack," Doug said excitedly. I'll trade you. I hear that usually comes with M&Ms or Skittles.

"Nope. I'll keep it," Mack said, still angered.

"Suit yourself," Doug said.

Mack was lost in his misery as he opened up his MRE and started pulling out the just-add-water heater to warm up his chicken and dumplings. So lost that he failed to notice that each member of the squad pulled out a PBJ from their own MRE bag that Dan handed to them.

Dan lost it first. He tried so hard to hold back a laugh that he spit part of his sandwich out.

"YOU GOTTA BE KIDDING ME? ALL OF YOU WERE IN ON IT? MY WHOLE SQUAD!" Mack was stunned.

Doug was laughing so hard that he fell off the gearbox he was sitting on and hit the one behind him with his head. It hurt, but it didn't stop him from laughing.

Heather walked by with Thor and noticed Mack fuming. "Good morning Mack," she said as she got closer.

"NO, IT ISN'T!" Mack roared.

"Well, you better carb up. I hear it's going to be a long day for you guys," Heather answered jovially.

Mack noticed that she had Thor's leash in one hand and a peanut butter and jelly in the other.

"Thanks for the PBJ!" Heather said as she just kept walking.

"That's it! I want a new squad!" Mack said as he got and walked away.

"Hey Mack," Earl called out. "Look under your bunk. You might find something where you left it!"

"Where did you guys hide it after you made the sandwiches?" Dan asked.

"It was under my bunk," Earl said. "A mere two feet from him during our interrogation."

"He'll feel better when he finds it back where it belongs," Evan said.

Earl and Doug started laughing again. "No, he won't," Doug choked out between laughs. "I put a finger hole in each piece of bread he has left."

"HEAD FIRST?"

Red Squad One backed their box truck up in front of the Montana. Work on separating the layers of the main part of the hotel had already begun as they jumped off with their packs and helmets and started making their way up the hill. Doug stopped and put his hand up over his eyes to shield them from the sun.

"Is that...?" he said, unsure of who he was looking towards.

"Who?" Mack asked, looking off in the same direction.

"I'm pretty sure that's Big Kenny over there," Doug said.

"Big who?" Mack asked, still not sure who Doug was talking about.

"Dude, you are such a city slicker. Big Kenny, you know–Big & Rich? Save a horse ride a cowboy" Doug started singing. "It has to be him. Who else wears a hat like that?"

They continued up to the top of the hill where they staged their gear.

"Hang tight here for a few fellas. I think that's the team from Spain up on the pile. I'm going to check in with them, that is if they speck-en-zie Deutsche," he said, purposely butchering the language. "I will talk to the backhoe driver too. Evan, you want to join me?" Dan asked.

"Will do. Let me grab my helmet."

Dan and Evan left as Doug, Mack, and Earl worked their way over closer to who they thought was Big Kenny.

"I'm sorry to bother you, but are you uh...are you Big Kenny?" Doug asked timidly.

He turned to look at Doug. "The hat give it away?" Kenny asked.

"Wow, I knew it was you from down there." Doug extended his hand. "My name is Doug, this is Earl, and this is Mack."

"Pleasure to meet you. You boys with search and rescue team from Virginia?" Big Kenny asked.

"Yeah. We are." Doug said with lingering stardust left in his eyes.

"I hear you are doing one hell of a job down here representing the Commonwealth," commended Big Kenny.

"I uh... well, I think everyone is doing the best they can for such a god awful situation," Doug said with genuine sincerity. "You mind if I ask what you are doing here. It's just...I really didn't expect to jump off the truck and see Big Kenny standing around."

Big Kenny stared off to where the track hoe was busy pulling large pieces of concrete from the pile and moving them away.

"I had a friend that was in there when the quake happened," Kenny said.

"Oh, I'm sorry to hear that," Doug answered sympathetically.

Dan and Evan returned and broke up the silence.

"No bueno with talking to the team from Spain, but pretty sure they are here making recoveries as well. I was able to communicate with the operator, though, and here is the deal. If there is a find, he will beep his horn and nest the bucket near the body. We will go up, try to make an I.D., bag the body, and then place it in the bucket. From there, the operator said he would lower it down off the pile where we can offload and place into a Stokes."

"Do we have a Stokes here?" Earl asked.

"We have an older, orange one in our truck, but there is another one already out by the pile. We'll just use it," Evan explained.

"Oh...Big Kenny, this is our squad lead, Dan, and assistant squad leader, Evan," Doug said, making the introductions.

"Pleasure to meet you, gentlemen. You're responsible for keeping this rabble in line?" Kenny asked with a sly grin.

"Pretty easy to spot, huh?" Dan replied with a smile.

"Well, that's the kind of boys you need to be doing this work," said Big Kenny.

"There's more truth to that than you might know," Dan replied.

The track hoe sounded its horn and rested its bucket. They all turned to see where it had stopped. On top of the pile, there were two members from the Spanish team working to remove debris from around a body. Evan looked around and didn't see any other members from their team.

"Doug, c'mon. They're going to need a hand." Evan urged.

They made their way to the top where they saw a male victim lying face down. One of the Spanish team members was struggling to get them positioned for the body bag, while the other appeared to be having just an all-around tough time with the situation.

Doug grabbed the arm of the Spanish rescuer that was trying to move the victim and held up a closed fist to stop what he was doing. Then Doug reached into his rear pocket and pulled out a wallet and found an I.D.

"One of ours?" Evan asked.

"No. Looks like he's a French national."

"Ok. Let's help them get him in the bag," Evan said.

"Evan, we need to be careful." Doug cautioned. "I mean, this guy is really bloated and could easily break open."

"Copy," replied Evan. They worked, tucking the body bag underneath the victim as much as they could, noticing small tears forming in the bag.

"Is this one of our bags?" Evan asked.

"No. This is a cheap plastic trash bag with a zipper," Doug answered.

The Spanish rescuer that Doug noticed was having issues started to retch. He pulled his mask off because he didn't want to vomit in it. After removing it, the smell overcame him, and he put it back on and vomited inside it.

Doug elbowed him. "Vamoose... Get out of here!"

The other Spanish rescuer motioned with his head for him to leave as well.

Having placed the victim in the body bag, Evan motioned to the operator to bring the bucket up behind them.

"Ok, Doug. I don't trust this bag. So I am going to lift the torso and have him take the legs. I'll leave you in the middle so we can guide him into the bucket over your shoulder. You good with that?"

"I'm good. Do me a favor, though, and find out what his name is in case we need to get his attention," Doug asked.

"Good idea," Evan said.

Evan looked over to the other rescuer. "Um...nom? Uh...nombre?"

"Ah, si. Sergio," said the Spanish rescuer.

Both Evan and Doug nodded.

Evan held a hand up to his chest. "Nombre Evan." Then he pointed at Doug. "Nombre Doug."

"Si...si. Evan and Doog," Sergio repeated.

"Close enough," Doug said under his breath.

"Sergio," Evan said, capturing his attention. "Uno, dos, tres, leven...?"

"I can't remember the word for lift," said Evan.

The Spanish rescuer nodded his head. "Si. Leventar...si." Evan pointed at the victim's legs. "Si. Leventar."

They all got into position, and Evan counted off. "Uno, dos, tres."

Doug grabbed the victim around the waist and lifted him to his shoulder while Evan hoisted the torso. He slowly let the bag move through his hands over his shoulder as the Spanish rescuer moved toward the bucket with the legs.

Just as Evan drew to the bucket with the torso, Sergio tripped and let go of the legs causing the body to bend in the bag at an angle. Doug felt the stomach break apart inside the bag. He instinctively stood up and let the rest of the body bag fall into the bucket over his back.

"Doug… you alright?" Evan asked.

He didn't answer. Doug just stood there.

Evan asked again. "Doug?"

"I think he broke apart in the bag," Doug answered, stunned.

"Ok…we can just uh…we can just double bag him when we get down with one of our bags," Evan said

"Yeah. That would be a smart thing to do," Doug answered.

Doug and Evan descended the pile as the bucket positioned the body for transportation to the morgue. Doug walked past Dan on the way to the truck to get a second body bag.

"You guys good?" Dan asked as Doug walked by with purpose.

"Fine. Need another body bag," Doug answered. Doug returned by them on his way to the bucket. "We can use another set of hands over here carrying him around to the morgue."

Mack shot up. "I got you."

They returned to the bucket where they helped Evan and Sergio place the victim into the second body bag. As they finished, three Spanish rescuers returned with the Stokes basket.

Sergio turned to his team and said something in Spanish and then turned to Evan.

"Evan, we leventar? Si?"

"What was that?" Mack asked

"He said he wants a peanut butter and jelly sandwich," Doug answered with a straight face. Evan paused to fight off a grin.

"Sounds like they are going to carry this one around," Evan said. "Si. Gracias."

Evan, Mack, and Doug moved back over to where Earl and Dan were hanging out with Big Kenny and waited for the next recovery.

The morning became afternoon as they took turns with the Spanish team making recoveries.

Earl and Mack positioned their packs up against a garden wall under a tree where they were able to sneak in a cat nap, while Dan and Evan continued a casual conversation nearby under a shade tree with Big Kenny.

Further down the garden wall, sitting in silence, Doug watched the track hoe as it continued to move piece after piece from the pile of death. He wanted to take a nap like Earl and Mack, but he was having a little trouble moving past the feeling of a body breaking open on him.

Doug jumped. He spooked at the sound of the horn. He stood, walking closer to the track hoe and looked up the pile to where the bucket had come to a rest. He saw a body, but what he was viewing didn't make sense to him. He took a few steps further up past the track hoe and stopped.

"I swear you cannot make this stuff up," Doug muttered.

Doug heard the door to the track hoe open up, and the driver started to get out.

"Stay in there, please. There's nothing you could do about it. It's not your fault," Doug said firmly.

The driver slowly got back in and closed the door. Earl walked up to where Doug stood.

"Did that just happen?" Earl asked.

"Yeah. Looks like he caught his neck with the edge of the bucket," Doug answered, scanning through the debris looking for a blood trail that might lead to where the victim's head came to rest.

"Hey, Doug, what do you say you sit this one out?" Earl asked. Mack and I just had a nice break. Go take a blow."

Doug sighed. "Walk with me, Earl."

They started up the pile, carefully placing each step they made. It was difficult to distinguish anything from anything. It was all concrete grey. Furniture, lamps, sheets, pillows, it was all the same dull grey color.

Doug spotted a short blood trail that disappeared right

before a small opening. He took a few more steps and looked down.

"Earl, I found it," Doug said.

Earl walked up beside Doug and looked down to see the victims head laying between to pieces of concrete.

"Earl, I'm going to stay right here. Do me a favor and go get one of our body bags. Make sure it's not one of those cheap things the Spanish had."

"Copy."

"And Earl..." Doug said.

"Yeah?" Earl answered.

"I'm going to tell you something, and I need you to accept it in the spirit that it is meant," Doug spoke.

"Yeah. Shoot," Earl said.

Doug was still looking down at the victim's head when he started to talk. "Don't use that psychobabble B.S. on me again about sitting out. We both came here to do a job, and we are going to do it."

Earl recognized he crossed a fine line with Doug, even if his heart was in the right place. "Doug, I'm sorry. I just..."

Doug cut him off. "No apologies. I know what you were trying to do, and I appreciate it. But again, we have a job to do, so let's do it."

Earl left to get the body bag and returned with Evan and Mack.

"Where's his...?" Mack started to ask.

"It's between my feet. I'll take care of this if you three can bag the body," Doug said.

"Mack, can you check his pants for a wallet or I.D. before we roll him," Evan asked. He checked what was left of his pockets and didn't find anything.

Doug stood silently below, waiting for them to finish. They carefully wrapped the body and turned it, so the zippered part of the bag was facing up. Afterward, they looked at Doug and said nothing.

Doug slowly bent over and grasped the head on both sides, lifted it, and placed it in the bag. Evan gave the signal for the bucket to come up so they could put the body in it.

They met the bucket at the bottom and transferred the body to the basket, carrying it around to the temporary morgue.

"This is just as bad, if not worse than the university," Earl said, looking at all the bodies stacked like cordwood.

They moved in further and set the Stokes basket down on the ground. They stood silent for a few moments as the four of them stared at the large number of dead victims before them. The smell of decaying flesh couldn't have been thicker.

"Do we know if we are putting them in here headfirst or what?" Mack asked.

They stopped and stared at each other, and then back at Mack.

"Mack, do you have a filter between your brain and mouth?" Earl asked.

"What?" Mack asked with a serious look.

It took a few moments to sink in, but the irony of what Mack said eventually caught up to him.

"No... I didn't mean it like...I meant..." Mack said, putting both hands on top of his helmet.

It was the first time any of them saw Mack embarrassed. Mack began laughing at himself, infecting the other three.

Gallows humor was very much part of their business. It was therapeutic whether they would admit to it or not.

Doug's mind drifted to a story that he often shared with fellow responders about a call he ran one time for a cardiac arrest. He was working as an engine medic out of Station 13. When they arrived on the scene, they were greeted at the door by a gentleman easily in his eighties. He led the engine crew to where his wife was sitting perfectly upright in her rocking chair. Doug knew she was dead, but he put her on the monitor just to make it official with an EKG tracing. After confirming she was in asystole (flatlined), Doug discreetly let his officer know so he could inform the husband.

"Sir, I'm sorry, but your wife has passed," Doug's officer said to the husband.

The husband just shook his head. "Can you speak up? I'm hard of hearing," he told the officer in a muffled voice common with people who have hearing impairments.

"Sir, your wife has died," the officer said a little louder.

The husband shook his head again. "I still can't hear you."

"Sir, your wife is dead!" the officer said, practically yelling at him.

"I thought so. She hasn't moved for an hour," the husband replied.

Doug had to put his hand over his mouth and leave the house to squelch his laughter. Through his very vivid and warped sense of humor, he pictured the old man scurrying about the house doing the various things old men do: like turning the thermostat up to a comfortable 107 degrees, looking out the curtains to make sure the neighbor's dog wasn't fertilizing his already well-manicured lawn, all the while wondering when his wife was going to get off the couch and fix his dinner.

As Doug's thoughts refocused on the scene in front of him, Evan made sure they had all the laughter out of their system before going back in public.

They made their way back up where the track hoe was still operating and placed the Stokes basket down where it would be ready for the next recovery. Dan was standing near the rear of the truck on the sat phone, entering something into the GPS as the others walked up.

"Ok, Chief. They're here now. We'll start heading that way."

"What's up?" Evan asked.

"The team from Martinique found a lady that is trapped but still alive, and they want us to go assist them any way we can. So, get your packs and load up." Dan could see a little pep in their step as they went to get their packs. He could tell morale was down a little bit, and he couldn't blame them for what they had to do the past two days. But, to a man, not one of them complained or even asked *why*. They just did their job.

"Hey, Big Kenny, we got to roll," Doug said, putting his pack on. "Another team found a live victim, and we are going to give them a hand."

"That's great news. You boys stay safe," Big Kenny said.

They all shook hands, and Red One walked back to their box truck and climbed in and sat facing backward.

"God bless you, brothers," Kenny hollered as Red One pulled away from the Montana.

"OUI, WE CAN HELP"

The day was getting late as their box truck slowly worked its way north. Doug passed out MREs and water to make sure everyone ate before getting to the next site. When the squad was at the university, they went the whole day without any food. It did not go unnoticed to Doug, but he knew that no one had an appetite, including himself.

Evan held his MRE in his hands while staring out the back of the truck. They slowed to work their way around a downed utility pole where he noticed a woman holding a baby with two small children standing next to her between two damaged structures. Evan hit the side of the truck twice with his hand, which signaled their driver to stop.

Evan stood up and looked out the back and did a quick survey of the street to make sure there was no-one else around. He knew what he was about to do could start a riot.

"Earl, grab a case of water and follow me," Evan asked. Both Evan and Earl climbed down from the back of the truck. Evan looked around a second time to make sure they were still not being watched.

"Doug, hand me a case of MRE's," Evan asked, pointing to the box beside Doug.

Doug stood up, grabbed a box, and handed it down to Evan.

Evan paused and looked at Dan before walking away.

"Discretely," Dan said.

Earl followed Evan over to the woman and children and set the water and MREs down beside her. Evan held his finger up to his lips, "Shhhhh."

She understood. "Merci," she whispered. "Merci."

Evan and Earl walked back to the truck and climbed back in. Red Squad One waved to her as they pulled away.

"You're a good man, Charlie Brown," Doug said to Evan as he watched the woman wave back, "Good man."

They drove on for another thirty minutes, where they reached a large crowd assembled in the middle of the road. The truck stopped, and Dan got up and looked out and saw two jeeps with UN guards behind sawhorse road barriers.

"I think this is it. Stand by for a second," Dan said. He hopped down and disappeared around the side of the truck and returned a few minutes later.

"Doug, a French doc up here wants to know if you can do an amputation," Dan said to Doug, as casually as asking to remove a splinter.

"No foreplay, huh, Doug?" Mack said.

Doug stared at Dan. "A French doc... wants to know if I can do an amputation."

"That's what he said. Hop out and follow me over," Dan answered.

Mack watched as the two of them walked away.

"Remind me to never complain about having a headache in front of Doug," Mack said as he made a slashing motion with his hand across his neck. "Zing...!"

Dan and Doug moved passed the barriers and worked their way through the crowd. Dan kept walking until they reached a middle-aged man standing next to the Martinique team.

"Doc, this is Doug, our medical specialist." The French doc turned and introduced himself in a thick accent.

"Ah, Oui," he said, extending his hand toward Doug. "Pierre...nice to meet you."

"Pleasure. Uh, Dan mentioned to me that you need to do an amputation?"

"Oui. A young female. She's stuck under a concrete column. Her right arm. You have equipment and medicine for amputation?"

"I do, but uh..." Doug said, stalling for help from Dan.

Dan knew that Doug did not want to insult Pierre, but

several more variables had to be contended with before getting to that point.

"Can you show us where she is? We would like to get a better idea of what else could be involved," Dan casually asked.

"Oui. This way," the doc answered in thickly accented English.

"Dan, let me go grab my pack. I'll meet you up there," Doug said.

"Ok," Dan answered.

Doug made his way back to the truck, past the bystanders and reporters with cameras and microphones.

"Mack, can you toss me my med-pack?"

Doug took his pack and turned to walk back, running straight into the reporter he passed moments earlier.

"Oh. Sorry" Doug apologized. "I didn't see you there."

"That's quite alright," a female with a British accent said. "I am a reporter with Aljazeera News. Do you mind if I ask you a few questions?"

"Sure, but just a few." Doug tried to step away. "I have to..."

"Oh wonderful," the reporter said, interrupting Doug.

"Can you tell me what your name is?" She asked.

"My name is Doug."

"And Doug, what is your last?" The reporter questioned.

"Dietrichson..."

"What a beautiful name. Scandinavian, I presume?" She asked.

"Norwegian..." Doug answered.

"Oh, how lovely," the reporter said.

Doug was cringing on the inside as he looked back at Evan, Earl, and Mack, who all sat with their arms folded, enjoying the show.

"Doug, where are you from?" the reporter asked.

"The team is from Virginia," replied Doug.

"And who sent you here, or did you come down here on your own?" The reporter questioned.

"No," said Doug evenly. "We are firefighters that work in Virginia, and we are members of an urban search and rescue team sponsored by DHS."

"Yes, yes. What does DHS stand for?" The reporter prompted Doug to reply.

"Department of Homeland Security," answered Doug.

"And that is who sent you?" she asked, pushing the microphone closer to Doug.

"Actually, no," Doug responded. "When we go out on international missions, we are sponsored by the State Department."

"Ok. That would make sense. Can you tell me what you are about to do here? Did I hear someone ask you to do an amputation?" The reporter eagerly pushed for answers.

Doug knew that's where all the questions were leading. "Without going into too much detail, we are here to assist the Martinique team," Doug answered.

"Can you be more specific?" the reporter asked, trying to pry more out of the interview than Doug was giving her.

"Actually, I cannot because I'm needed elsewhere; however, we have a public information officer here with us that will be more than willing to answer a few more of your questions," Doug responded matter-of-factly.

"Oh, brilliant. Thank you so much," replied the reporter.

"Sure. No worries," Doug said with a polite smile. "Mack here is our public information officer and has a great wealth of knowledge that he is willing to share with you." Doug shot Mack a sly grin and disappeared around the side of the truck to go find Dave.

Doug met back up with Dan, who was standing between two buildings with Pierre and other members of the Martinique team. "What took so long?" Dan asked with a miffed look.

"Later…" Doug replied, looking down to see where the victim was trapped.

A Haitian female laid face down with her right arm extend out and trapped under a concrete column. On top of her was a rod iron fence attached to a metal gate that was being pushed down by concrete.

Dan and Doug knew it was going to be challenging to get her out. Not impossible, but difficult. It would take time to cut through the gate and fence without it collapsing on top of her.

"Pierre, do you know what her name is?" Doug asked.

"I believe they said it was Esther," Pierre answered.

"Has she responded to you yet?"

"She is in and out of consciousness and will moan from time to time, but no purposeful responses that I have seen."

"Ok. Dan, you got a second?" Doug asked.

Doug turned and walked back out to the street with Dan. "The amputation is the absolute last thing we need to do," Doug said.

"I know. We have hours of work ahead of us," Dan agreed.

"Before we cut her arm off though Dan, do you think we can try and dig underneath that column to see if we can free it first? I mean, I know it's dead after being there that long, but at least the amputation could be done in a cleaner place than she is right now."

"I thought about that, but look at all the weight that is pushing in from the outside. If we cause even a small shift, its 'game over,'" Dan said.

"Speaking of 'game over,' did you notice the building behind us?" Doug asked, looking through the Martinique team to a turquoise color building.

No more than five feet away from where they would be working to rescue Esther, there was a three-story building that should have collapsed during the quake, but it didn't. Its top two stories extended out past the first and formed a porch that was supported by pillars. The pillar closest to where the team would be working was broken, causing a very precarious lean of the top two floors.

"Yeah. That actually will be priority one. Let's go back and get the others so we can talk this through.

Dan and Doug arrived back at the truck, and much to Doug's delight, the reporter was gone.

"Hey, that was pretty quick, Doug. Did you use a chainsaw this time?" Mack asked

"No comment. You need to go see my public information officer," Doug replied with a wink.

Dan took a moment to scan the immediate area to see who was within earshot. Behind the barrier were several

TV crews and reporters with mics on booms pointed in their direction, hoping to catch any soundbites.

"Alright, guys, listen up because I am not going to talk that loud for obvious reasons. First off, we are here to assist them; however, it doesn't look like they have the tools they will need to get this done. So, that likely means we will become more involved as it progresses. As soon as Doug completes the amputation, we will place her in our stokes, and everyone with an American flag on their shoulder will take a step back and let the Martinique team carry her out. Everyone copy?"

The squad understood what Dan was saying and acknowledged him. Dan continued. "Before we get started, the building next to us is ready to drop, and I'm not sure why it hasn't yet. One of the things that they have, and we don't is some shoring. We'll use that to shore up the porch as best we can and just take it from there. Dan paused for a few moments looking back towards the rescue site.

"Tools...We have a rod iron fence on top of her along with a metal door. I'm thinking an air chisel, Petrogen torch, and eventually the chipper when we get to the concrete column. We need to chip just enough away, so Doug has room to do his thing. You will have to use it close to her head, so we need to be steady with it. Any questions?"

"Enough talking. Let's get to work," Earl said, jumping down out of the truck.

Red One started making their way back up to the site

so they could begin shoring as another French physician stopped Doug.

"Are you the medical specialist for the American team?" He asked Doug, giving him a once over from head to toe.

He was younger than the other physician and spoke with such a thick French accent he could have been the French soldier from Monty Python and the Holy Grail.

"I am. Do you need a hand with something?" Doug answered.

"I was told that you would be the one to assist with me with the amputation. Oui?" The physician questioned.

"Help?" Doug asked a little taken back. He had to stop for a second and remember what Dan had just told them. They are there to assist.

"Sure, Doc... I can assist."

"You have supplies? Bone saw?" He asked, making a sawing motion with his hand across his arm.

As he was talking, Doug noticed that he had a tourniquet in his hand. "Yes, I have a bone saw, but..."

He interrupted Doug. "You have medicine? Drugs to sedate?"

Doug held his hand up. "Stop."

"I have a bone saw, but there is no room to use it," Doug explained.

Doug took his pack off and set it on the ground and pulled out a sealed package and showed it to the Doc.

"We'll use a Gigli saw," Doug said, holding the bag up.

"Ah, Oui. Oui. Gigli," he said as he took it from Doug and placed it in his hand with the tourniquet. Doug reached down and snatched it back out of his hand.

"That is the only one I have with me, and when it is time, I will give it to you."

"Time?" the doc repeated.

"Oui. Time. We have a lot of work to do before we amputate. Perhaps hours. I'll keep you updated."

Doug knew that the Gigli would probably be safe with him, especially with the death grip he had on the tourniquet that he was holding. But just the same, it was his equipment and supplies, and it would stay with him. He excused himself as politely as possible and joined the rest of the squad.

PEPÉ LE PEW

Red One spent the next thirty minutes shoring up as much as they could with what they had. Back in the US, they would have used wood to make their own shoring. One, it was readily available and could be cut to specific sizes; and two, wood shores creaked when they were put under a heavy load or stressed and served as a good indicator that it was time to get out of where ever they were in a structure.

"Hey, Doug, got a second?" Dan asked.

Doug turned and saw Dan standing between the buildings looking down at Esther. Doug passed off his shore to Earl and made his way over through the crowd.

"I just talked to Pierre. Did that other French doc find you?" Dan asked.

"Are you talking about Pepé le Pew?" Doug quipped. "Oui, he found me."

Dan laughed. "Well, keep your cool and help him out with whatever he needs."

"Copy, but my gear is staying with me. If he is around when the time comes, I will pass off what he needs, but not until then," Doug said firmly.

"Fair enough," Dan replied.

Pierre approached Dan with the team leader from Martinique when they were finishing a conversation in French. "Dan, this is the Martinique team lead, Leif. He wants to know if you have any metal cutting tools."

Dan looked at Leif and nodded. He assumed that Leif did not speak English and told Pierre that they had an air chisel and a gas cutting torch.

Pierre turned to Leif and translated what Dan had just told him. During the translation, Leif looked at his team and back at Dan. Afterward, he relayed another message back to Dan through Pierre. "He says that his team is not trained to use that equipment and would like it very much for you to help."

"Oui. Oui," Dan said with a smile, shaking Leif's hand. Dan turned to Doug. "We're up. Go grab the air chisel and meet us up by Esther. I'll send Earl back for the torch."

Red Squad One wasted no time getting to work, and it didn't take long before running into their first hurdle. The metal door was heavier than they realized and was too thick for the air chisel, so they attacked the hinges with the cutting torch. Earl cut the hinge furthest away from Esther first and then went to work on the second one. This would allow them to catch the gate as it dropped free from the second hinge and be lifted away from Esther.

They got a scare while cutting the second hinge when hot slag from the gate dropped down and ignited trash next to Esther. There was momentary panic because there was nothing they could do to reach the fire. One of the members from the Martinique team ran out to the street and scooped up dirty water in his helmet and tried to douse it out, but it wasn't enough.

Doug didn't know if it would work, but he ripped open his pack and spiked a liter of IV fluid and placed a pressure bag on it. "Mack, Earl, lower me down headfirst so I can get under the gate with this." They looked like a couple of schoolyard bullies trying to shake lunch money loose from an unsuspecting book nerd.

"Lower!" Doug yelled out. Doug had a hard time because he couldn't use his hands to brace himself. He used one to aim the IV at the fire. The other one had to keep pumping on the airbag because as fluid came out, the pressure in the bag would decrease. It took every chest and abdominal muscle he had to get turned in the right direction to get the fire out.

"We're good. Pull me up," Doug finally said. Doug stood back up and felt the blood rush out of his head and got a little dizzy, enough he didn't know Doc Bruce was standing next to him.

"You alright?" Bruce asked.

"Yeah, I'm fine. Just a little unsteady from standing on my head."

"Right. Keep an eye on your guys working through this

one, because it looks like there will be a lot of that when you get to the concrete."

"Will do Doc," Doug answered.

Without notice, Pepé le Pew wedged his way in between Doug and Bruce and looked down at Esther with his tourniquet still in hand. "You are ready? Oui?" The physician interjected.

"No, we are not ready," Doug said firmly. "We will let you know. Get back."

Pepé le Pew left them as Bruce pulled Doug back away from everyone else.

"Are you alright?" Doc asked.

"I'm fine, Doc, just tired," answered Doug honestly. "But you better keep him away, or I swear I will put that tourniquet around his neck."

Hours passed as the team worked to free Esther. Their efforts gave Doug enough room so he could get an intraosseous IV started in her left shoulder. Intraosseous IV infusions were lines that go into bones, established using a specialized drill. Although they are not the first option, it was easier with the limited access they had.

Evan, Earl, and Mack started working on the cement column that was on Esther's arm. One would operate the chipper while the other caught the debris from dropping onto her head, and the third would take a break. They continued that rotation until there was enough room to complete the amputation.

"Evan, if you can, I need you to make your way back behind her and look underneath the fence to make sure there is no entanglement on her legs before we do this," Dan asked as he kept watch from above.

Evan carefully made his way to the side of the trench they formed by removing as much of the rod iron fence as they could, and worked his way back several feet.

"Dan, her legs are clear. She should be able to slide out when we are done."

"Ok, Evan. Doug, are you ready?" Dan asked.

"I'm giving her Ketamine now. Dan, if you want to go track down that French doc," Doug directed.

"Ok. I'll be right back," Dan said, going off in search of the French doctor.

Evan crawled back out with a hand up from Doug. "Doug, you need anything from me," Evan asked, giving the scene a once over.

"Not really," replied Doug. "Just keep people back. Oh, we need the Stokes basket up here. I think it's still on the truck."

"Right. I guess that would be helpful," Evan quipped.

Dan returned with Pepé, his presence alone giving Doug a bad rub. Doug felt like he spent the whole time pacing around getting ready for a prize fight while they worked their asses off. And it wasn't so much that he was the one that got to do the amputation, Doug already got that t-shirt. It was more that it was for a notch in his belt and not out of compassion. "You ready, Doc?" Doug asked.

"Oui. Ready," answered the doctor.

"Alright. Go ahead with the tourniquet, and I'll pass you some sterile water and betadine to clean her arm," Doug calmly directed.

"She's sedated, Oui?" Pepé replied.

"Yep. Ketamine," Doug answered. He carefully stepped down and placed the tourniquet on her arm and then used the sterile water and betadine to clean the site where he would cut. Doug watched him work efficiently, which gave him some redemption in Doug's eyes...some.

"You ready for the scalpel?" Doug asked.

"Oui. Ready," Pepé replied.

Doug pulled the scalpel out of his pack, unsheathed it, and passed it to the doc.

The French doc made one long incision around the arm as much as he could and switched to the other side where he was able to finish it. Esther made no sound or movement. He continued making the cuts deeper and deeper until he reached the bone and separated the muscle and fat away so he could get a good visual of what he had to do next. He handed the scalpel back to Doug in exchange for the Gigli saw he had ready for him.

Less than a minute later, the amputation was complete. When Pepé was done, he stood up with a triumphant expression, just staring down at his work.

It was obvious that it wasn't just Doug that got rubbed the wrong way by him.

"You done? Earl asked in his growly voice.

"Oui. I'm done," the French doc answered.

"Then get the hell out of the way," Earl barked, grabbing his arm and pulling him out of the hole.

"Mack, hand me the Stokes so Doug and I can put her in it."

Earl and Doug reached down and pulled Esther free, placing her in the Stokes and passed her to the Martinique team. The Martinique team, and the Martinique team alone carried Esther out to a cheering crowd.

Doug stayed back a few moments and scanned the area to make sure he left nothing behind. As he got up to leave, he looked down where Esther laid and saw a little toy army soldier with a parachute.

MERCI

He walked out from between the buildings and through the jubilant crowd, making his way back to the truck where he came to a stop, not believing what he saw. "They didn't! No way!" Doug was livid.

They did. In the back of the box truck, unattended, Esther lay in the Stokes basket while the celebration was taking place in the street.

Doug scanned the area for anybody from Red One without success. In fact, he wasn't able to see a team member anywhere. He climbed up in the back of the truck to get a better view of the crowd. "Is that Doc Woolwine?" Doug questioned aloud.

"Doc Woolwine," Doug yelled out.

Doug could see that Doc Woolwine heard his name being called, but wasn't sure where it was originating.

Doug waved his hands in the air. "Over here! Grab your pack!"

Doc Woolwine ran up to the back of the truck. "What do you need, Doug? He asked.

"We need to get her the hell out of here. Stay here so I can go find Dan," Doug said, starting to get pissed off.

"Yeah. I got it. Go!" Doc instructed.

Doug jumped down from the back of the truck and looked back toward the street barrier. He spotted Dan talking to one of the UN guards in their jeep.

Doug pushed his way through the crowd with force to reach him. "Dan, they left Esther in the back of our truck."

"What?"

"I said they left Esther in the back of our truck by herself!" Doug shouted.

"No, I heard you. I'm just confused why they left her there," Dan said.

"I'm going to take her to that Israeli field hospital they were talking about," Doug said.

"That's an hour away, Doug!" Dan exclaimed.

"You have a better idea?" Doug asked.

"Even if I did, they are not going to let you go without force protection," Dan argued.

"Dan, I'm going with or without it."

Dan said nothing. He just stared at the two UN guards in the jeep.

"Can I just take one of these guys?" Doug asked.

"That's what I'm thinking; we just need to use some tact," Dan considered.

"Dan, we don't have time for tact. Hey UN guy, I need one of you to come with me to the hospital," Doug ordered.

The UN guard Dan was talking to looked at Doug, having taken no offense to his abruptness.

"Oui, you can take him," he said, pointing to the guard in the passenger seat.

"Merci," Doug said, walking over to the other guard and tapping him on the shoulder. "C'mon...Pepe, you are coming with me."

"Hey Doug, not everyone from France is named Pepé," Dan said, only half-seriously.

"Oh, yeah?" Doug said. "But their names start with a P. We have Pompous, Petulant, Prick..."

"Alright, Doug. That's enough," Dan said, cutting him off.

The guard had a confused look on his face.

Doug tapped him on the shoulder again. "C'mon, let's go."

The other guard shooed him out of the jeep.

"Hey Dan, Doc Woolwine is coming with me. I'll meet you

back at the BOO," Doug said as he walked away with the guard in tow.

Doug took the guard and placed him in the passenger seat. "Buckle up!"

"Bookul up...?" The guard spoke in confusion.

"Never mind," Doug said, shutting the door.

Doug jumped into the back and pulled the door down as the truck drove away. He knelt beside Esther to make sure the tourniquet was still controlling the bleeding.

"Doug, we need to get a line in her," Doc Woolwine said, looking over Esther.

"She has an IV in her left arm," replied Doug.

"Well, if she did, it's not there now," Doc noted.

"It must have been pulled out when she was extricated," Doug answered.

Doug positioned himself by her head on the right, and Doc Woolwine sat on the other side.

"Doug, I see a good external jugular on this side if you want to give it a shot," Doc observed.

"Yeah. I will. Do you mind spiking a liter for me? I should have one left in my pack," Doug said.

"I have two liters; I will use one of mine," Doc Woolwine answered.

"Thanks, Doc." Doug turned Esther's head to the right and turned on his helmet light. "Can you hand me an alcohol prep, Doc? He asked. It took three preps to get the dust and dirt off of Esther's neck before he was ready to start the IV.

Doc handed him an 18 guage. "I figured that was the size you wanted."

"You read my mind, Doc. You should be a medic," Doug joked.

Doc Woolwine laughed. "Not me. That's too much like work."

Doug positioned himself the best he could, and just as he was ready to break the skin, the truck hit a pothole, and everything in the back went flying.

Doug and Doc Woolwine could hear the driver apologizing from the front. Doug had the truck come to a stop before making a second attempt at the vein.

"Nice one, Doug," Doc said, handing him the IV.

"Thanks," said Doug, taking it from him.

"Do you want her on the monitor?" Doc asked.

"Yeah, I just forgot. Do you mind doing that Doc while I clean her arm and get a dressing on it?" Doug asked.

"Consider it done," Doc answered.

Doug dumped a whole bottle of betadine solution over

the stump that remained on Esther's right arm. He then placed a trauma dressing over the open end and finished with a pressure dressing.

They kept tabs on Esther as they continued to make their way to the Israeli field hospital. She started to move, and her pulse and blood pressure started to go up as well.

"Doc, do you think she is trying to wake up because I am out of vitamin K?" Doug asked, watching the monitor.

"Probably." Doc Woolwine replied. "Do you have any Fentanyl you can give her? That should hold her until we get there."

"I should have one left," Doug answered. Doug pulled out his narc kit when the truck came to a stop, and he could hear the driver speaking to someone.

A few seconds later, he heard a knock on the back roll-up door.

"You have to open it from the outside," Doug yelled. "Doc, can you give her the Fentanyl while I deal with whatever this is?"

"Sure," Doc said, taking over seamlessly where Doug left off.

Doug could hear whoever was outside fumbling around with the door latch trying to get the door open. The longer it took, the angrier he got.

The door flew open, and Doug saw two guards standing there with rifles.

It was obviously a security check. Doug could tell by the way they were looking around in the back. "Hey! We need to get to the hospital! Do you speak English? Hospital...!"

The two guards looked at each other, then the one who opened the door said something in French.

"ARE YOU DEAF? I DON'T SPEAK FRENCH! CLOSE THE DOOR!" Doug yelled at them.

Doug reached up with his hand and started to close it down, and the guard stopped him repeating what he said in French.

"Inspector Clouseau, we need to get her to the hospital!" Doug yelled at them as he bent down and waved Esther's stump to get their attention.

The guard's gaze froze on what Doug was showing them.

"Yeah, now you're getting it!" Doug said, standing back up to close the door again.

This time the guard was actually helping him close the door and didn't realize he was pointing his rifle at Doug.

Doug slapped the end of the rifle away from him. "You better point that thing in another direction before I go guillotine on your ass with this door."

The door was quickly closed and latched, and they were once on their way again.

Doug sat back down, shaking his head.

"French..." Doug said as he looked over to Doc Woolwine, who sat motionless with his mouth gaped open.

Their truck backed up to the entrance of the field hospital, where two nurses met them, helping to unload Esther and move her onto a triage stretcher. Doug helped as they carried Esther to a small tent that was attached to a larger one.

Doug stood by as they started their own assessments. He was impressed at how efficient they worked, and even more impressed at the equipment they had for being a field hospital.

"Did you bring her in?" someone asked, walking up beside Doug.

"Uh, yeah," Doug said without turning to see who he was addressing.

"Oh, yes, sir. I'm sorry, Colonel." Doug said, realizing that the physician was also an Israeli military colonel.

"We removed her arm about an hour ago now with scalpel and Gigli. We used Ketamine for sedation, and her vitals have remained stable. She started to wake up as we were arriving. We administered Fentanyl, and she has received a total of liter normal saline. Other than the isolated injury, that's really it. Her chest, abdomen, pelvis, and legs are all grossly intact."

"Well done, well done. By the way, you needn't worry

about my rank. It was nice you noticed it, but we are all just friends here trying to do the best we can," the Colonel said.

The Colonol watched Doug as the nurses worked on Esther. He could tell he had been through a lot in a short period of time.

"You need rest, my friend," the Colonel said.

Doug kept staring straight ahead. "I'm sorry, sir, what..."

The doctor physically turned Doug so he could look at his face. "You need rest, my friend. And this needs rest too, he said, gently prodding Doug's head. "You need to rest your mind as well."

Doug chuckled. "Is it that noticeable?"

"Mm, more than you realize," he calmly noted.

"I will, sir. I promise," Doug responded.

Doug stayed a few minutes more to watch them work and thank them all for being there and the great work they were doing and then started to leave. As Doug began to turn and walk away, he stopped. "Colonel, I think this belonged to her," he said. "Can you please see that she gets it when she wakes up?"

Doug handed him the toy he found after Esther was extricated.

"I will. I will give it to the nurse right now," the Colonel answered.

"Thanks again," Doug said, extending his hand.

"You're welcome," the Colonel said sincerely.

Doug turned to leave the triage tent and stopped to look into the main part of the field hospital that was lined with twenty or more patients. Many of the patients were missing legs and arms, and some were missing both.

His eyes traveled from bed to bed and stopped when he noticed a young Haitian female that was missing her left arm at the shoulder. A woman sat next to her reading. It was Liezel.

Doug started walking slowly toward her bed so that he could get a closer look at Nadine. Liezel looked up and immediately noticed him.

"Oh, it's you. It's her guardian angel," Liezel said as she quickly stood and went to hug him.

She squeezed him tightly. Doug was at a loss for words, gently returning her hug.

Liezel released him and wiped tears from her face. "Please come see her. She will want to meet you."

"No. Please let her rest. I don't want to bother her. She needs to rest," Doug insisted.

Liezel would hear nothing of it. She pulled him by the arm over to the side of the bed, and she returned to her chair. Nadine was sleeping with her head toward her mom.

"Sweetie, Sweetie, someone is here to see you," Liezel said softly to Nadine, squeezing her hand.

Her eyes twitched as she stirred and tried to focus on her mom.

"Nadine, Doug is here," Liezel prompted. "The one who got you out of the university."

She turned her head to see a blurry view of Doug that slowly came into focus.

Doug looked down at Nadine and was struggling to fight back his emotions.

Nadine studied Doug and saw that he matched the silhouette that looked over her the day she was rescued. She let go of Liezel's hand and started to move it slowly toward Doug. He recognized what she was trying to do and reached down and grabbed her hand.

Grabbing Doug's hand, she slowly pulled it up to her mouth and kissed it. "Merci...merci," Nadine whispered.

Tears started coming down Doug's face as he took his helmet off with his other hand and placed it in the chair beside him. Still holding Nadine's hand, Doug leaned down and kissed it. "You're welcome, Nadine."

Doug stood and gathered himself the best he could, walking out of the field hospital. As he left, he saw a small grove of trees where he sat and gave way to the flood gates, no longer in control over his own emotions. He sobbed, unsure if it was because Nadine was alive, or if it was just a cumulative effect of everything he had experienced. He didn't care, though. Deep down, he knew it was coming, and it needed to be squared with. As Doug sat trying to process his emotions, another truck arrived at the field hospital.

"Thanks for the lift, Blue squad," Dan said as he and the rest of Red One jumped out. They walked up to the field hospital and past the truck Doug arrived on, where the UN guard still sat in the front seat, unbuckled.

They all walked into the tent and looked for Doug. The Colonel noticed them as they entered.

"Are you looking for your medic?" he asked.

Dan turned. "Yes, sir. He brought the young lady in with the amputated right arm."

"I think you will find him out resting by the trees," guided the Colonel.

"Good. Thank you, Colonel."

Dan looked into the larger tent on his way out, where all the patients lay in their beds, spotting Liezel.

"Something wrong, Dan?" Evan asked as Dan stared at Nadine.

"Nope. We're good. Let's go find our medic," Dan replied distractedly.

Doug sat in silence with his head resting back against the tree. He reached up to wipe away a few more tears and was distracted by shadows standing next to him. He looked up to see Dan, Evan, Earl, and Mack staring down at him. He felt embarrassed, but he didn't see judgment in their faces.

"I uh... went in there to drop off Esther, and uh...looked in the hospital tent and saw her..." Doug said, his voice trailing off.

He had to pause and look back down away from the squad. "I didn't think she would, uh...survive, you know?"

They said nothing. They didn't have to. Just standing there was all Doug needed.

He cleared his throat and tried to regain his composure. "I'm sorry to wuss out on you guys. It just...it all caught up to me," Doug tried to explain.

"Doug," Earl said in the sincerest growly voice any of them ever heard from him, "There ain't no wusses out here with me tonight, and don't you ever forget it."

Doug reached out his hand, and Earl lifted him to his feet as Doug smacked him on the helmet.

"Guys, I think it would mean a lot if we all went in there so she could see everyone that took part in getting her out," Doug said, putting his helmet back on.

"I think it's a great idea. But uh...there's something we need to know before we go in there," Mack said with a serious face.

"What?" Doug replied.

"Did you really smack a rifle away from a French guard and tell him you would go guillotine on his ass?" Mack asked disbelievingly.

"You heard about that already?" Doug said with a shy grin.

"Yep," Dan said. "Doc Woolwine called me on the sat phone to give me a situation report after you got here."

"Well, it seems like you guys already got the goods on me, but yes, I told a French guard I would go guillotine on his ass after I slapped his rifle out of my face," Doug admitted.

AMAZING GRACE

It was the first time in almost three weeks that the whole team had been together since they arrived in Haiti. They were being demobilized and flying back to Virginia the following day, but they still had a lot of work ahead of them. Their whole cache was being donated to the people of Haiti. Tools, generators, tents, radios, medications all had to be inventoried. Doug assisted Doc M. and Doc Bruce with the medical cache as they made their delivery to the WHO.

Earlier in the day, Red One delivered a tent and a generator to a group of physicians to be set up and used as an operating room. They were happy to be involved in more humanitarian efforts. It allowed them to clear their heads and relax from their constant obligation to heightened situational awareness. They were not worried about aftershocks shifting a building and collapsing on them, or what would happen if they moved this piece of concrete versus another one.

The highlight of the day came as Doug was helping Mack move some supplies into storage at the embassy and came across a brand new, sealed container of Gatorade.

"Oh yeah, baby! Gatorade," Doug said excitedly.

"I would have traded my PBJ for this a couple of weeks ago," Mack said, stashing it under his BDU shirt. "I won't tell if you won't."

"Tell what...?" Doug asked.

"That's right," Mack answered.

That evening, Chief Tobias gathered the whole team together for a quick hot wash from each squad along with any lessons learned. The squad leaders took turns detailing their more difficult rescues as they shared what worked and what didn't.

When it was Dan's turn, he walked through the process of tunneling back to Claudette at the Montana, and how voices heard in pipes could be a very misleading as an indicator as to where a victim could be located. As he continued talking, he was distracted by the team members standing behind the rest of the squads that caused him to shift gears on the fly.

"You know, guys, I have to stop and think about everything we had to use to make these rescues happen. You know our chippers, jackhammers, generators, cutting torches, ropes–hell, everything. As many tools as we kept breaking, logistics just kept fixing them while rehabbing the rest of our gear and getting us back out the door. Loggies, on behalf of the squads, you did one hell of a job, and we thank you."

The whole team raised to their feet and gave the Loggies a thunderous and well-deserved standing ovation.

Later that night, an Army chaplain led a prayer service for the whole team. It wasn't mandatory, but when the task force leaders tell you that it isn't, and if you have been around long enough, you know otherwise.

The team settled into their respective squads as the chaplain stood up and led them in one verse of Amazing Grace. As they sang, everything around them fell silent. Embassy staffers close enough to hear stopped what they were doing to listen. No noises from the other side of the embassy walls could be heard, only the words of Amazing Grace.

The chaplain let the silence linger before he started speaking. "John 15:13 tells us that 'greater love has no man than this, that he lay down his life for another.' I don't necessarily believe that the apostle John meant literally dying for another as Christ did for you. Although, from what I have been told, there are a couple here tonight that gave it a good effort."

A soft chuckle spread throughout the team as Earl and Mack elbowed Doug, who was sitting between them.

"What I am talking about is what you did here with the life in your body. The past three weeks of your life here, the incredible risks you took, the compassion and love you showed to the people of Haiti, that part of your life will remain here. You laid it down here, and here it will stay.

Whether you believe in God or not, the men and women of this team showed the greatest love in our Maker's eyes."

The chaplain looked out over the team, taking time to look at every member directly in the eye.

"When you stop and look back at your lives and think about the steps that led you here to this very moment in time, do you think it was all by chance. Look around you. Look at the team member sitting next to you. Think about all the individual life decisions that had to be made by every person on this team that brought you here together. The reason that you are all here together, now, is because you were meant to be. You were appointed to be here by the Almighty so you could lay down your lives for others."

"Hmm," Doug whispered, but not so softly, Earl couldn't hear him.

"What is it?" Earl whispered.

"Nothing... it's just something Jackie said to me before we left. She told me exactly what he just said. She said, 'I was appointed for this.'"

The chaplain led them in a closing prayer, and squads all got up to go back to their separate tents.

"Fellas, unless you want one last MRE, I can make us some peanut butter and jelly sandwiches," Mack said.

"And...?" Doug asked.

"And what?" Mack asked.

"What do we have to go with it?" Doug prodded.

"Oh, yeah! Doug and I scored some Gatorade today." Mack exclaimed.

"That's what I call fine dining," Earl said, putting his arm around Mack's neck.

Red One went back and plopped down in their bunks while Chef Mack worked his magic. They started to relive the past three weeks. They laughed at Mack asking about putting bodies into the morgue headfirst, and Earl yanking him to the ground when they heard gunfire, and how freaked out Doug must have been during the aftershock at the Montana.

Doug sat up on his cot as the conversation started to trail off.

"Earl, is this what it was like when you were a Marine?" He quizzed.

"How do you mean?" Earl replied.

"Well, you know, when you watch military movies, and you see guys in their squads and the bond they have – that sort of thing," Doug tried to explain, not sure if Earl knew what he meant.

"Listen, Doug, we all have been away from home for a spell, and we all miss our wives, but what kind of bond are we talking about here, sailor?" Earl answered.

They all laughed.

"I know what you are getting at Doug, and here is the deal. We all know each other from the department and would consider each other friends. However, it's not like we all go to each other's kids' birthday parties or go on vacations together and stuff like that. But Doug, I will tell you this though, this will forever bond us. I am not trying to sound all dramatic and everything, but it's a bond that comes from a shared, intense experience. That's what we went through here. It's a bond that was forged by fire, and unless you experience that fire together, with that shared understanding of what we went through together, it doesn't happen. We came out of the fire together, and a bond was formed. I feel it, and unless these guys want to BS you, I know they do too."

"Earl," Dan said, "you sir, are a warrior poet. I don't think any of us could have put it better."

Dan stood up and raised his bottle of water mixed with contraband orange Gatorade.

"Gentlemen, I am proud to have served with each of you on Red One. I wish this were alcohol, but cheers!"

"Cheers," the rest of Red One said, raising their orange mixed drinks.

BROKEN HEART AND A BAND-AID

The Virginia Urban Search and Rescue Team touched back down at Dulles airport. The pilot taxied their chartered 737 between two crash trucks that sprayed water over the aircraft from both sides in big arches in honor of their return.

"Hey Mack, did you put your thermals back on before we flew out of Santa Domingo?" Dan asked, looking out the plane's window. "The board of supervisors and press look pretty cold out there."

"No. Oddly enough, I didn't think about it in the 100-degree temps we had," Mack answered.

The team exited the plane, where they did a brief meet-and-greet with the press and local politicians on the tarmac. Then, they made their way onto chartered buses for the quick escorted trip by the police motorcycle squad.

At the fire academy, Jackie was parking her E350 land

barge. "Ok, kiddos, let's scoot. We want to be in there before Daddy gets back."

They all jumped out and grabbed each other's hands, along with the welcome back signs they made and walked into the academy where all the other family members awaited the team, along with more press and local politicians.

"Jackie, over here," Doug's oldest brother Donnie said, waving his hand to get her attention. Donnie gave her and the kids a big hug.

"I hope you don't mind me coming. He was there for me when I came back from deployments in the Air Force, and I thought it would be nice to be here for him."

"No. Of course not. He would want you here," Jackie reassured.

He knelt down and pulled Jessica, Eric, Gabe, and Susannah close. "You know that your Daddy is a hero? He saved lives over there in Haiti. You make sure you give him big hugs when he gets here, ok?"

"Ok, Uncle Donnie," Susannah said.

Jessica looked at the sign she made. "Hugs," she echoed.

Jackie and Donnie visited while they waited for the team. Jackie smiled as Donnie talked about everything the team did while in Haiti, and how he saw Doug on CNN and other clips. She could tell he was proud of his little brother.

Moments later, the motorcade announced their arrival with blue lights and yelps of their sirens. Everyone in the academy started cheering.

One by one, the team members stepped off the bus and made their way through the crowd looking for their own family. Doug was stuck in the middle of the pack and couldn't find Jackie in the large crowd.

"Doug! Doug! Over here," he heard Donnie yelling. As he got closer, he was able to spot Jackie and the kids. Donnie took a step back, so they had time together.

Doug dropped to his knees and got one big hug from all the kids. "Hey, munchkins! I missed you all so much," Doug said, giving them all a big squeeze.

Jessica held up the sign she made for Doug. On top it said: We missed you, Daddy. Underneath that was a picture she drew of two hearts. One was broken and separated into two halves. The other heart showed the two halves fitting back together being held together with a band-aid.

"Schmoopie, you made that for me?" Doug exclaimed. "It's beautiful. Thank you so much. Can I have the world's biggest fish kiss?

Jessica closed her eyes and pushed her lips out as Doug did the same thing.

"That was the best one ever!" Doug said excitedly.

Doug stood up and gave Jackie a big hug and kiss, followed by a hug from his big brother.

It didn't take long before a reporter approached Doug. "I'm sorry, but do you mind if I ask you a few questions? It won't take long. I don't want to keep you from your family.

Doug appreciated the tact she used as opposed to being cornered by Aljazeera the way he was in Haiti. "Sure. I have a few minutes."

"Can I start with your name?" she asked.

"Doug Dietrichson," he answered.

"And Doug, what do you do with the team?" She questioned.

"I am a medical specialist," Doug replied.

"Overall, can you tell me what the experience was like being there so soon after the earthquake?" The reporter quizzed.

"To begin with, it was heartbreaking. It's tough to see so many in need, and that is a huge understatement. There are so many people that literally have nothing left. No family, no home, no food, no water. Nothing. As a rescuer, it was a non-stop assault on all five senses, but I really don't want to go into those details right now."

The reporter scribbled as fast as she could to keep up with what Doug was saying. "Ok, wow, that was pretty succinct. I don't suppose you can really say anything more."

"No. I think that just about sums it up," Doug answered.

"Again, thank you, Doug. I'll let you get back to your family," the reporter replied considerately.

"You're welcome."

Doug turned back to his family and Donnie. "Who is hungry? I am starving for real food. Donnie, you in for dinner?"

"No. You need alone time with the family," Donnie answered.

Donnie gave him another hug. "Good job over there, little brother. Proud of you. I know Dad would be too."

"Thanks, big brother," Doug nodded.

They finished saying bye to Donnie, then Jackie put her arm around Doug.

"Let me guess, you want to eat at Artie's, and you are going to order the hickory grilled Angus with the calamari appetizer."

"I was thinking kielbasa with mac and cheese," Doug answered sarcastically.

"Uh-huh," Jackie said, swatting Doug on the bottom.

Twenty minutes later, they made their way to Doug's favorite restaurant. The parking lot was full.

Doug pulled back out on the main road and backed in next to a hydrant.

"Seriously?" Jackie asked.

"It's fine. You have a department sticker on the back," Doug said carefree.

"It's a fine that I am worried about," Jackie cautioned disapprovingly.

"C'mon, we're good," Doug said, pulling her toward the doors.

They were able to be quickly seated where Doug let Jackie order for him.

"Perfect, babe," Doug said.

The waitress returned with drinks for the kids and Doug's calamari. Then unexpectedly, she sat a draft ale down on the table.

"I'm sorry, I didn't order that," Doug told the waitress.

"I know it came from the gentleman over at the corner table. Should I take it back?"

Doug turned to see a gentleman he did not know raising his beer for a toast.

"He wanted me to tell you welcome home," the waitress said, looking back over to the man raising his glass.

Doug picked up the beer and returned the toast and took a big long drink.

"Doug, you're still in uniform?" Jackie reminded him.

He set his beer down and looked at her. "It's not the front porch, but I guess I could strip down right here."

They both had a good laugh.

Doug looked at Jessica across the table and asked if she would say a prayer for dinner. She immediately folded her hands and started to pray.

"Dear Lord, hat..," she suddenly stopped.

Doug peeked through his right eye to see what the hang-up was. Jessica sat perfectly still with her eyes closed, and her hands still folded.

"Dear Lord," she started again. "Dad will not take his hat off..."

Doug snatched his ball cap off his head. "Sorry, Schmoopie."

Jessica's prayer was her usual, with an added extra blessing for the "broken hearts in Haiti," just like her sign showed.

After a long and relaxing dinner, they all made their way back outside, where attached to the windshield was a ticket.

"So much for that sticker, Doug," Jackie chided.

"Wow. That's a first. It's not like I am completely blocking the hydrant. There's plenty of room for them to connect if they had to."

Doug walked over and yanked the ticket out from under the wiper. It was folded in half so that the front could be seen, but there was no writing on it. Doug turned it over.

Nice parking job ace. Missed you at the academy. Congratulations on a job well done. Mark.

Doug shook his head with a big smile. "Cops..."